SMILIN' JACK

and the

Daredevil Girl Pilot

A New Story Based on the
Famous Comic Strip by

ZACK MOSLEY

Authorized Edition

WHITMAN PUBLISHING COMPANY
RACINE, WISCONSIN

TABLE OF CONTENTS

LIST OF ILLUSTRATIONS

Jack Martin Had Never Seen So Much Fog

SMILIN' JACK
and the Daredevil Girl Pilot

CHAPTER ONE

THE MYSTERY GIRL

A gray, shadowy mist floated between the cabin of the plane and the little red and green lights gleaming on the wing tips. Fog, clouds and mist: this was the worst weather Smilin' Jack Martin had seen in many a hop in his speedy, custom-built cabin ship.

An ocean of murk crowded between Nashville and Memphis—maybe it ran all the way north to St. Louis, perhaps over the whole Mississippi valley. Jack had never seen so much fog stuffed into one place.

Somewhere under the plane—and Jack knew from his instruments that he was right side up—was the world. But it wasn't wise to try to land on it during a night like this. It was unwise to do anything except try to fly out of the fog or let the fog get out of the way of the flier.

But certain things might make landing a necessity— one was Jack's gasoline supply.

To all of Jack's senses it seemed he was alone in the universe with a drying gas tank. His instruments told him he was at five thousand feet, high enough to be safe from hills, but comparatively low if his gas ran out. He might come down quickly, and the world is unkind to planes without gas on foggy nights.

"I ought to have better sense," Jack upbraided himself. "The weather report said I'd meet bad weather over Tennessee, but I never thought it would be as bad as this."

To preserve his self-confidence, Jack reminded himself that his flight was not due altogether to a lack of good judgment. "Downwind" Jaxon had told him to stop in Omaha, on his way West to be inducted as a Coast Guard officer. To go off to war without saying good-bye to an old pal like Downwind was unthinkable. So Jack had flown out of his way in spite of bad weather reports.

"This fog is just what the Japs ordered—regular Fifth Column stuff," Jack decided. "It's likely to wreck one perfectly good Coast Guard reservist."

It couldn't be helped, so Jack quit beefing. The fog was getting thicker anyhow. Nashville had reported zero-zero, which meant the only thing to be seen there was fog, on the ground and in the air.

If that was the way it was, Jack couldn't land in Nashville. Maybe Memphis!

Smilin' Jack lifted his "mike" to his lips.

"Smilin' Jack callin' Memphis!" he said. "Callin' Memphis! How's your weather, Memphis? Come in, please."

The receiver emitted a coughing *pwop* as Jack cut the transmitter and waited for the reply.

"Hello, Smilin' Jack," it came. "Memphis is zero-zero-X. Can't even see the boundary lights 'cross the field here."

Wasn't the fog ever going to let up? Jack glanced at his fuel tank gauge and groaned aloud. It was zero-zero-X, too, like the ceiling and visibility at Memphis.

"Thanks, Memphis." Jack spoke again in his transmitter microphone. "I'll try up north—probably at Cairo."

Cairo, Illinois, might as well be Cairo, Egypt, as far as being within range of Jack's fuel supply, but he might make it if the tail wind shoved him hard enough. He hung up the microphone. Soup! This stuff wasn't soup, it was solid granite. This thick fog could have been cut into blocks and used to build courthouses and libraries!

The compass swung around as Jack headed northward. He listened to the faint buzzing sound in the radio receiver. That would be the St. Louis beam.

No it wasn't a radio-beam buzz. It was a humming sound—almost musical. What was the matter with that radio? Was it "going haywire," or was the beam catching boogie-woogie?

The noise in the receiver grew louder.

"Da-da-da de-dee-dah! Ump-pum-de. De-dee-day! Floogie-woogie floy floy."

Now what in the world was the matter with that radio beam? Was the radio gummed up by this soup? Once more came the refrain:

"Da-da de-dee! Gogie-wogie floy-floy-flogie."

Of course it might be an angel. A modern angel though! Maybe Jack himself was crazy. Maybe the beam was all right. But it certainly didn't sound all right.

"Da-da-hut-sut! Da-da—"

Jack had to put a stop to this before he went completely off his *mental* beam. But wait a minute, there was a human note to that sound. It wasn't a beam at all, but somebody singing! It was a girl!

Jack growled and picked up his mike.

"Listen, Miss Floy-floy!" he said sternly. "Get off this wave band with your floogie-woogie. I've got things to do to keep from wrapping up my plane."

"Oh!"

The singing ended with a startled gasp. There was a slight pause and then came the station identification in a melodious contralto.

"Oh, I'm so sorry!"

"You ought to be!" Jack spoke before he thought.

"It's my transmitter," came the voice again, apologetically. "It slipped out of its regular wave band and I didn't even know it was on. I was just humming to myself—it's so foggy up here—"

"Up here? Are you flying, lady?"

"Why, of course, silly! Did you think I was sitting in my plane on the ground? I'm flying and I felt so alone in the world, I guess I just got to singing to keep from feeling lonesome—"

"Lady," Smilin' Jack said, with considerable restraint, "your transmitter is still on. And I've got my opinion about anyone that goes for a joy ride in soup like this. Now if you'll just turn that little switch and get off the air, I'll get on the radio beam so I can get out of trouble.

Every minute you wait means that my gasoline is getting that much lower. I'm in plenty of trouble."

"Trouble? Oh, I'm so sorry! Maybe I can help you."

"Yes, lady, you can help by getting off the air. Now will you please—"

"But where are you? Your signal is strong. You must be awfully close. If I could only find you I could help you."

"Help me?"

Say, maybe she could. She certainly couldn't hurt much.

"Well, it won't hurt to try. I'm north of Memphis on the St. Louis beam. If you can help me out, you can sing the rest of the night, Miss Floy-floy."

"So generous of you—Mr.— Grumpy!"

"I'm Smilin' Jack Martin!"

"Smilin'? You certainly don't sound smiling to me, but keep talking. I'm getting your signals clear now and you ought to be pretty close."

"Don't run into me. My landing lights are burning, but you won't be able to see them very far away."

"That's fine. Just keep talking. I think I'm real close now."

"Lady, do be careful! You're likely to smash into me. Your signals are awfully loud."

"Oh, I see your lights! Here I am, over to your right!"

Jack turned his head around and his eyes widened in complete amazement as he saw, almost at the tip of his wing, another machine flying in the same direction as his. A cabin monoplane, with sleek lines and a powerful motor—an expensive job!

But this was only half of what Jack saw. The cabin was brightly lighted and a girl was at the controls of the other plane. An angel after all, thought Jack. And a modern one indeed! Even at this distance he had a revelation of a soft, smiling face and glorious hair. The girl smiled and waved at Jack.

"Don't gawp, Smilin' Jack," came her voice over the radio. "I'm a perfectly natural phenomenon—a girl flying a plane. Now then, if you're in trouble, we can't waste time. You said your gasoline was low."

"Low! Lady, the gauge said the tank was empty fifteen minutes ago. I don't understand how the motor keeps going. It's likely to stop any minute now."

"Well, I know where there's a little landing field near here—"

"There was one at Memphis, but it was too foggy to use," Jack said.

"Oh, but this one is behind a hill and there's an updraft that usually makes it clear even on foggy nights. The field has lights and it's large enough for your plane. Can you follow me?"

"If I can't, I don't deserve to be rescued," Jack said. "What do you think this is, my first solo?"

"I'm banking right, Smilin' Jack!"

With a wave of her hand the girl put the plane into a turn. Smilin' Jack followed the maneuver with admiration in his eyes. This girl was a crack pilot and she handled those controls like a veteran.

Precision flying was one of Smilin' Jack's specialties and he had no difficulty in holding his aircraft within sight of the girl. She was going down now. Suddenly the planes came into a hole in the fog.

"Here it is, Smilin' Jack! The updraft clears away the fog here!"

Below his plane, Jack saw the lights of a farmhouse perched on the side of a hill.

The girl gunned her motor, running the prop at low pitch so that it gave a resounding roar, loud enough to awaken farmers for miles around.

"That's my signal," the girl explained by radio. "Mr. Dayfield will turn on the airport lights from his house."

As she spoke, floodlights suddenly flashed on directly below the planes. They lighted a small "postage stamp" size field on the gentle, sloping approach to the hill.

"This is my private field," the girl explained, "but you can use it. You've got to stop quickly, though, or you'll go through the fence into Mr. Dayfield's garden."

She was circling now, and preparing to land. Jack lowered his flaps and checked his speed. His troubles weren't over yet, for the field was tiny and Jack's craft had a high landing speed. He side-slipped and dropped toward the lighted field.

As the wheels of Smiiin' Jack's airplane touched the ground, his motor coughed and died—the last drop of fuel was gone. Jack applied his brakes and flipped his tail around so that the plane came to a stop not twenty feet from the fence that cut the flying field off from the farmer's garden.

But the girl, who had been headed for a landing, zoomed upward and disappeared into the fog on the other side of the field.

"So long, Smilin' Jack!" came her voice in Jack's earphones. "Sorry, but I can't stop. I've got a date on the West Coast tomorrow!"

"Thanks a million!" Jack shouted into his own microphone. "You've saved my life, Miss Floy-floy—say! What in the dickens *is* your name?"

Her reply was a melodious laugh.

"I'll tell you some other time!"

"Hey! Wait!" Jack called. "You can't run off and leave me like this. I owe you a lot. I want to contact you again later so I can really thank you. What's your name?"

"I can't stop now, Smilin' Jack!" she called back. "Mr. Dayfield will sell you airplane gas and put you up for the night and that should solve all of your current problems. So I'll toddle along. Seventy-three!"

"Don't go away!" Smilin' Jack pleaded. "Hello . . . hello . . ."

No reply came over the receiver. The girl was gone. She had switched off her transmitter. Who was she? What was she thinking of, flying around in a foggy night like this? She could at least have given Jack her name.

But Jack couldn't figure out the answers just sitting there. The farmer was coming through the gate onto the airfield. Mr. Dayfield, she said his name was. Jack

Jack Landed on the Tiny Field

climbed from his plane to meet him.

"Howdy, son!" the farmer hailed. "Foggy night, ain't it?"

"Your fog-proof field certainly was a lifesaver for me," Jack said. "I'm plumb out of gasoline and if that girl hadn't shown me the way here I'd be cracked up along the river."

"Oh, so Betty brought you here?" he asked. "I thought I heard another plane but I reckoned she was already well on her way to the West Coast—a friend of hers cracked up in a plane out there a few days ago."

"Betty? What's her last name?" Jack asked.

"Betty Brown—she goes to Charterfield Girls' School in Memphis when she ain't gaddin' around the country in her flyin' machine," Mr. Dayfield said. "Well, what shall I do for you? Do you want a place to stay for the night?"

Jack considered the question. If he got enough gas he could fly out of the fog.

"No, just give me some gasoline. I'm flying to Omaha."

The farmer motioned toward a gasoline pump at the edge of the field. Jack walked to the pump and picked up a can. He'd have to get enough gas to taxi to the pump.

"Where's Miss Brown going on the West Coast?" Jack asked.

"Valley Ridge. What do you want to know for?" There was a twinkle in the farmer's eyes as he asked the question.

"Oh, I thought I might run across her some day and thank her for saving my life."

"Oh, is that it?"

In a few minutes Jack had refilled the plane and he was ready to start.

The engine caught and Jack waved to the farmer. Then he took off, his thoughts centered on his recent narrow escape.

At least Jack knew her name was Betty Brown—the girl, not the escape—and she lived in Valley Ridge, California. There might be more than one Betty Brown there—probably there were thousands of them in the United States—but only one particular one he had to find. Jack felt sure he would find her.

First, though, he had to stop in Omaha to see Downwind.

When Jack landed at the airport the next morning, he found Downwind had been waiting all night for him.

"What kept you so long, old-timer?" the red-haired Downwind Jaxon asked.

"The worst fog I've ever seen!" Jack explained. "And I ran out of gasoline right in the middle of it, but—"

"Humph! So you let weather get the worst of you, eh?" Downwind grinned. "That's the first time a little soup ever got in your way. You're slippin'."

"It was more than 'just a little weather!'" Jack insisted. "Honestly, Downwind, it was terrible! If it hadn't been for Betty—"

"Betty?" An understanding glint crept into Downwind's eyes. "Oho! Now I see what grounded you. Betty! Now there's an excuse for being late. You ain't slippin', Jack. I apologize."

"Don't get me wrong, Downwind!" Jack laughed at his friend's kidding. "Betty saved my life and then sailed away without even letting me get a good look at her. But I think I can find her on the coast—"

"Oh, sure!" Downwind grinned. "We'll just wire Tojo and Hitler to hold up the war a couple of months until you locate Betty and thank her for saving your life. Shucks, Jack. You got other things to think of. There'll be plenty of cute little de-icers on the Coast. Just thank them and what's the difference? Betty got as much kick out of saving your life as you got out of having it saved."

"Not quite, Downwind," Jack laughed. "Well, perhaps you're right. This is war and there's a lot of nasty business to be done. I can look up Betty after the war, when she'll probably be married to some dodo who tended the anti-aircraft gun in her front yard."

"Sure! You can repay her by sinking a couple of Jap subs. What does she look like?"

"Why, I'm not sure because I didn't get a good look, but I could recognize her plane anywhere and her voice is one I'd know in a million—melodious, low, beautiful —like—well—like an angel's—"

Suddenly a plane's motor roared and across the field a small cabin ship taxied for a take-off. Jack's mouth dropped agape and he stood staring at the plane.

"Downwind!" Jack cried. "There's Betty Brown's

plane now! It's taking off from this airport."

Jack broke into a run across the field, but the swift little cabin plane already was sailing upward into the air. Smilin' Jack waved and shouted, but the plane nosed west without even a circle around the airport.

Jack slowed down to a walk, then dejectedly returned to Downwind who was standing with his hands on his hips, looking disgustedly at his pal.

"I thought you weren't interested?" Downwind asked.

"Kid me if you want to, Downwind," Jack replied, "but with me a debt of gratitude can't go unpaid. I was simply trying to thank her."

"Well, Jack, it's been nice seein' you again. I know that I'd lose your friendship keeping you here when you ought to be flying out to California to thank an angel-voice," Downwind said. "Your plane's oiled and gassed and if you hurry you might pick up the angel trail near Salt Lake. So long, pal. Sink a sub or two for me."

Grinning sheepishly, Jack shook Downwind's hand.

In virtually no time at all, Smilin' Jack was in his plane winging his way toward the Rockies. But Jack and Downwind had underestimated the speed of the small cabin plane. Jack did not sight it all the way to the Coast, although he sent his own ship along at a three-hundred-mile-an-hour clip most of the way.

In the early afternoon Jack set his plane down on a field near the navy airport in San Diego. He reported at once to Commander Young, who was in charge of Jack's Coast Guard squadron.

"Oh, yes, Martin," the officer said. "We sent for you because we need you on a special job—something out of the ordinary for the Coast Guard. You are to report to Mr. Stevens, but he was called out of town today and he won't be back until tomorrow. Why don't you just take some time off, and see San Diego and report back here tomorrow—that's when you're scheduled to be here anyhow."

"Good idea," Jack said. "How far is Valley Ridge from here?"

"Valley Ridge?" The commander eyed Jack strangely. "About fifty miles. Why do you ask?"

"I know a young lady there," Jack said. "I thought I'd call on her."

"Oh!" the commander nodded understandingly, and quickly gave Jack the proper directions.

Later in the afternoon Jack landed his plane at a pretty little airport just outside the town of Valley Ridge.

Several other craft were on the field, but one of them attracted Jack's attention immediately. It was a small cabin monoplane with a powerful motor.

There was no mistaking that plane! It was exactly like the one Betty Brown had flown. Since this was Valley Ridge, the plane should be hers—

CHAPTER TWO

IN DUTCH

Jack bounded out of his own plane and started toward the other craft. On the far side he saw a small figure approaching—a girl with black hair, sparkling eyes and pretty teeth. She was swinging a helmet on her arm as she approached the plane. Jack mentally noted that she was more beautiful than he had expected.

Jack walked around the plane and came face to face with the girl. He touched his cap and smiled. The girl's eyes searched him curiously, apparently failing to recognize him.

"Beg pardon," Smilin' Jack said sheepishly, "but aren't you Miss—er—Miss Floy-floy?"

Her eyes widened incredulously. The astonishment which swept over her face lasted only a moment; it was replaced by a warm smile. Betty laughed aloud and, at the sound of her voice, Smilin' Jack knew he had made no mistake in the girl's identity.

"Smilin' Jack!" she exclaimed. "How did you get here so quickly? I never thought we'd meet again—or at least not so soon!"

"I was afraid we wouldn't meet very soon," Jack admitted, "and I wanted so much to see you again—to thank you for saving my life. But I recognized your plane the minute I landed here, Miss Brown."

"Oh, you know my name? But of course Mr. Dayfield told you."

"Yes, he told me and he said you lived in Valley Ridge," Jack explained. His eyes turned admiringly toward Betty's sleek plane. "Some job you have there."

"Custom built. Father had it made for me," she said.

"Your father—"

"I'd offer you a ride," Betty went on, not giving Jack a chance to ask who her father was, "but I'm terribly upset right now. A friend of mine has been in a bad accident and I flew clear out here from Memphis to see him. Now that I'm here I understand that no one will be permitted to visit him for several days—"

"Him? Your brother?" Jack asked. "Or your father?"

"Neither," Betty replied. "My fiancé."

Jack glanced quickly at her left hand. For the first time he noted that there was a diamond on her ring finger. Someone else had discovered Betty before Smilin' Jack.

At the sight of the diamond, Smilin' Jack became speechless. He wanted to ask questions. He wanted to see Betty again. He had a thousand things to say. But he found that he could say nothing.

With considerable effort he thanked her again for saving his life and watched her climb gracefully into the cockpit of her plane. As the little ship rose briskly into the air, Jack suddenly realized that Betty was gone, leaving him very much alone in the center of a vast airport.

Not quite alone, however, he instantly became aware.

From the side of the field, two men appeared, walking snappily toward Smilin' Jack. They were strangers, so Jack turned to go back to his plane.

"Hey, wait a minute, buddy!" one of the men, the taller of the two, called. "We want to talk to you!"

The shorter man broke into a run and Jack noted a glint of metal in his hand. As the man came closer Jack saw that he held a gun.

"Say!" Jack blurted angrily. "What *is* this?"

"Don't try anythin' funny, Powder!" the short man barked. "I've got you covered an' I'll blast you out by the roots if you make one false move."

Perplexed, Jack waited for the men to reach him, unable to understand what part he played in this melodrama.

The taller man stood in front of Jack and flashed a badge which he held in the palm of his hand.

"FBI," he said, as if that explained everything. "Come along with us, Powder. This is the end of the line and you're under arrest—we've been looking for you a long, long time. We thought we'd find you when Miss Brown dropped in."

So Betty Brown was mixed up in this too!

"Come along, Powder!" the G-man told Jack again, with finality.

"Say!" Jack exclaimed suddenly. "What did you just call me?"

"'Powder.' Would you rather we called you *Mister*

Pellet?" the short G-man asked sarcastically.

" 'Powder' isn't my name. You've made some mistake. I'm Smilin' Jack Martin."

"Aw, tell that to the Marines!" the taller man scoffed.

"Listen! I'll tell it to the Coast Guard instead. I've an appointment with Mr. Stevens tomorrow and he'll wring the FBI's neck for this!"

"Ho! I'll say you've got an appointment with Mr. Stevens," the short G-man chortled. "Only he hasn't anything to do with the Coast Guard. He's our chief in the FBI."

Confused, upset and considerably angry over his unjustified arrest by the federal officers, Smilin' Jack went along with his two captors to a small car. He was ordered into the back seat with the taller G-man and the machine whisked him away toward the business section of Valley Ridge. Halting beside a three-story building, Jack was taken from the car and led up a stairway to a tidy little office on the top floor.

Here they waited silently in a small reception room. The G-men watched Jack much as a cat eyes a goldfish in a bowl. After a short delay a connecting door opened and a well-groomed man walked briskly into the room.

"Hello, boys," he greeted the two G-men. "What have you got here?"

The newcomer was about average height, with sleek black hair and a closely cropped mustache. His sharp eyes seemed to pierce Jack with a glance. After inspecting the prisoner, he looked inquiringly at the men who had taken the aviator into custody.

"We finally caught him, Mr. Stevens," said the taller man, nodding his head at Jack. "He was at the airport talking to Betty Brown. We recognized him from his pictures."

"Yeah, chief," the smaller man added. "This is Powder, all right."

"Powder?"

There was a note of incredulity in the voice of the man addressed as Mr. Stevens. Was this the man Smilin' Jack had been called by the Coast Guard to meet? What did the FBI have to do with the Coast Guard Reserve?

Stevens' eyes were scanning Jack more closely than ever. Nodding approvingly at something he saw, he let his lips curl into a pleased smile.

"You'll do, all right," he said. "What's your real name, young man?"

A new note in Stevens' voice made Jack feel easier.

"I'm Smilin' Jack Martin, Mr. Stevens," Jack said. "I was called from the East by the Coast Guard—"

"Smilin' Jack Martin!" Stevens interrupted. "This is better than I expected." He turned to the two G-men and waved them toward the door. "All right, boys. Leave this man with me. I'll take care of him."

The shorter man's mouth flew open in surprise.

"But he's dangerous, chief!"

"If I need help, some boys in the next room can handle him," Stevens said. "You did a nice piece of work, both of you."

"What's nice about it?" Jack asked himself—but not aloud—as the two men left.

Stevens watched them go and then turned to Jack.

"Well, Smilin' Jack," he said, "you've got your credentials with you, I suppose?"

Jack reached inside his pocket and brought out his pilot license and Coast Guard Reserve papers which he handed to Stevens.

"I tried to show them to your two officers," Jack said, "but they wouldn't give me a chance."

"They're both new to the FBI and a little green—but hard workers," Stevens explained, glancing at the credentials, satisfying himself and handing them back to Jack. "Yes, I guess you are Smilin' Jack, all right."

"I had an appointment for tomorrow with a Mr. Stevens," Jack said. "But I thought it was in the line of duty with the Coast Guard—not the FBI—"

"I'm the Mr. Stevens you were sent to see," the sharp-eyed man declared. "Sorry my men made the mistake of misinterpreting you, but it gives us a whole day's start on our program."

Jack mopped his brow with his handkerchief. Being arrested by federal agents in wartime was no fun, even though Jack knew he could prove his innocence.

"I'm still in the dark!" Jack said, smiling.

"Your resemblance to a man called Powder is remarkable," Stevens said. "But how does it happen you know Betty Brown?"

Betty Brown! Why was *her* name always cropping up?

"Your Resemblance to Powder Is Remarkable!"

Why was *she* being watched by the FBI?

"Oh, I only met Miss Brown yesterday," Jack explained. "She helped me out of some trouble in a fog near Memphis. I heard she lived in Valley Ridge and I hopped over here to thank her. I met her just as she was leaving, at the airport."

Stevens nodded slowly.

"You'll have to give us the details so we can check your story, Jack," Stevens said. "You see, we can take no chances. Miss Brown is one of the reasons we sent for you. You see, she is a spy suspect!"

The words slapped at Jack's ears like a crash of thunder.

"Why—why it can't be true!" Jack exclaimed. "She's not the type."

"Unfortunately spies often do not look the type," Stevens said. "We may be wrong and we haven't much evidence against her except that she associates with others whom we are certain are spies. We have been watching her, and through a slip-up my men arrested you because you looked like one of those known spies. Luckily, the man you resemble already is in custody, although my men do not know it. We've been keeping that fact a secret for a very special reason."

Mr. Stevens paused while Jack digested the words.

"As long as you're here now," the FBI man went on, "I think we can get down to business. You're the only man we could find—in the Coast Guard, the Army, the Navy and the Marines—who can do this very special job—"

"You flatter me, Mr. Stevens," Jack said. "I take some pride in my work, of course, but I'm surely not the best pilot in the world—the armed forces are full of men as good as or better than I."

"It isn't your ability as a flier, Jack," Stevens explained. "It's your appearance. You see, your picture in the Coast Guard files led to your selection for the job I have for you."

"Yes?" Jack wondered vaguely if this was a gag about his well-known smile.

"Yes."

A humorless twist of his lips flicked beneath the little close-cropped mustache. Mr. Stevens was all business. There was no fooling now. Something very important was afoot, for he was talking to Jack in tones unmistakably serious.

"Come—I'll give you an idea what's to be done," Mr. Stevens said, opening a small closet door and taking his hat from a shelf.

The FBI operative led the way through the corridor and down the rear stairs. He motioned for Jack to get in a small car that was parked behind the building. The car swung out of the driveway onto a boulevard.

"This spy ring we're investigating," Stevens began, as he drove the car, "has been operating in both North and South America. We haven't been able to bag the leaders but we did shoot down one of the higher-ups—a fellow named Dave Pellet, who is called 'Powder' Pellet."

"The man that looks like me?" Jack asked, suddenly guessing the answer.

Stevens nodded.

"Yes. Powder wasn't badly hurt, but we managed to convince the physician on the case that he shouldn't see visitors. In that way we have kept his arrest a secret. He's in the hospital now, but he doesn't know he's guarded. We're going to see him, you and I."

The car swung up the drive of a large brick building. Stevens stopped the machine and climbed out, followed by Jack.

As they entered the building, the familiar odors of a hospital assailed Jack's nostrils.

Riding an automatic elevator to the third floor, the two men followed the hallway to the extreme end of an ell of the building, where Stevens stopped and opened the door.

Jack stepped into the room. To his astonishment, the room was empty.

"Say, what *is* this?" Jack asked in surprise. "A joke?"

"Sh-h!"

Stevens put his finger to his lips and moved softly across the room to a small panel. He opened the panel, exposing a little glass window.

"Powder is in the next room," Stevens explained. "We had this line-up glass window put here so we could keep our eyes on him without being seen. It's one-way glass: we can look through it without his seeing us."

"Oh!"

Jack had heard of this kind of glass. He looked through the panel. On a hospital bed in the next room lay a sleeping man who was about Jack's age, build and height, except that his hair was curly, while Jack's was straight, and it was also blond while Jack's hair was dark. The sleeping man's face was paler than Jack's wind-tanned skin, and he wore a small mustache.

Jack turned to Stevens.

"Do I look like him?" Jack asked.

"Not exactly," Stevens explained, smiling. "But your measurements are the same. That can mean a great deal. Your eyes are the same color, your ears and nose the same shape as his, you are approximately the same age, height and build. I've conferred with several Hollywood make-up artists and showed them your picture. They say that you can be made into a perfect twin of Powder in no time at all."

Jack peered through the glass again.

"He's just a rat as far as I can see," he remarked with a shrug of his shoulders. "One of those handsome rascals who are no earthly use except to cause trouble. I've known a lot of men like him—you can pick them out the minute you see them—but I never thought I looked like one."

"You really don't, Jack," Stevens said. "After all, it is largely the expression that makes the character show up in your face. The expression on Powder's face can be mimicked by you with a little practice and then the movie make-up men will do the rest."

"So I'm to do some undercover work in this spy ring, disguised as Powder?" Jack asked.

"You've guessed it," Stevens said. "Now that you've had a look at Powder, let's go back to the car where we can talk without being overheard. I'll tell you more about what you're to do. If you accept—?"

"Don't kid me," Jack cut in simply.

A few minutes later, as the car whizzed along a country road, Stevens explained the assignment he had planned for Smilin' Jack.

"Powder didn't have an ordinary accident," Stevens explained. "Our men shot down his plane. He was knocked out and didn't have time to destroy certain documents which identified his connection with the spy ring and gave us some important plans. Among the papers we found was a letter instructing him to meet 'The Head' three weeks from today off the coast of South America. This man referred to as 'The Head' is, we believe, the chief of the spy ring."

"Whew! That would be a haul if you caught him."

"*When* we catch him, Jack."

"It's our chance to wreck the enemy's entire espionage system, providing we learn The Head's future plans and where his bases in this hemisphere are," Stevens said. "That's why we want you as an undercover operative to meet The Head, learn these things and let us know before we arrest him. It's likely to be the most dangerous job you've ever tackled, Smilin' Jack."

"You're wasting time," Jack returned shortly.

Jack felt cold chills running up and down his spine—not from fear, but from the realization that here was a task which had odds against success from the very start. Literally millions of obstacles lie in the path of any man who tries to impersonate another. An impostor can easily be detected in spite of the most perfect disguise.

But although Smilin' Jack realized he was taking a long shot, his chances were no worse than many an American soldier was taking without complaint on the fighting front. Any service a man could perform for his country in this day of grave peril was a simple duty that he could not hesitate in undertaking.

"You're our man, Smilin' Jack," Mr. Stevens asserted. "Now I'll take you back to my office where we'll map our campaign from start to finish. We'll do everything in our power to make you a perfect twin of the man you're to impersonate."

"Yeah," Jack said with his ready smile. "Including going to a beauty parlor for a bleach and a permanent wave. That's gonna be hard to take, mister."

Stevens chuckled, but there was little mirth in his face as he turned to Jack with a serious expression in his sharp eyes.

"Yes, Jack, but there's something that may be harder to take," he said. "There's a mark on Powder's left hand—a symbol of some sort that appears to have been burned in the flesh with a branding iron."

Jack nodded.

"Okay," he said.

"Perhaps we can duplicate the mark with acid," Stevens continued, "but it won't be fun."

"Well," Jack said slowly, "I hope I can take it. What has to be done, must be. Just one slip-up in my disguise and I'd be a dead duck."

In this business there could be no half-way measures. He had to do everything possible so that his disguise would be perfect. The more perfect the disguise, the more chance the desperate plan had of succeeding.

CHAPTER THREE

LIFE AND DEATH REHEARSAL

The days that followed were busy ones for Smilin' Jack.

The branded symbol—a flaming sun crossed by a flash of lightning—was successfully burned in acid. But the wound was so painful that Jack could not use his left hand for some time.

Then came those uncomfortable trips to the beauty parlor for a permanent wave and a hair bleach. Jack's mustache sprouted and the make-up artists set to work trimming his hair-line and applying padding to his clothing so that nothing was left undone to make Jack resemble Powder.

Stevens and a corps of experts who studied Powder day and night brought up new things each day for Jack to master. For instance, Powder had a taste for a special brand of strong cigars. Jack himself rarely smoked cigars. Learning to enjoy Powder's kind of tobacco was almost as much punishment as the branding ordeal.

Records were made of Powder's voice during his conversation with his nurse and his physician. Jack listened to these records and spent hours copying Powder's enunciation, pronunciation and inflection.

"That guy uses better English than I do," Jack admitted to Stevens.

"Well, that's about the only improvement you'll get out of this masquerade," Stevens said with a small smile.

"Skip it," Jack retorted.

As his hand started to heal, Jack moved into the hospital room adjoining Powder's, so that all of his spare time could be spent studying the spy and his mannerisms.

"You have to talk, walk, eat and sleep like Powder," Stevens stressed.

This was more difficult than it sounded. Powder seemed to like the very foods that Jack detested. Powder plucked his eyebrows and Jack found that this was a painful operation. Powder slept with his mouth open and snored, and learning to snore is no easier than breaking the habit.

But, one by one, the problems of learning a lifetime of habits in a few days' time were overcome. Jack worked hard to copy the numerous distasteful characteristics of the spy. He spent hours memorizing the personal items found among Powder's effects and studying out clues to Powder's individuality. The one thing that bothered Jack was the lack of data as to the spy's associates and past.

"I wouldn't let it worry you too much, Jack," Stevens pointed out. "Men in Powder's line of business don't talk much about their past life or their associates. He's probably pretty much of a stranger to the men he directs."

Eight days of constant rehearsing had completely changed Smilin' Jack's manner and appearance. Jack was walking up and down the hospital room practicing his

Jack Became More Like Powder Every Day

role when Stevens, watching near by, spoke sharply:

"Powder, come here!"

Jack turned quickly without thinking.

"Yes? What is it, Mr. Stevens?" he asked.

Stevens smiled appreciatively and Jack grinned from ear to ear. He *was* Powder—he had answered to the name unhesitatingly. The disguise was perfect.

"Atta boy, Jack!" Stevens exclaimed. "I was just testing you. You responded as if Powder were the only name you're ever known. You're Powder to a T, now!"

Jack was pleased by this praise, but still not confident.

"I'm glad you think so," he said, speaking in Powder's voice. "But that's only your opinion. I'd like to test my disguise on someone who has known Powder. I may be Powder to you, but would I pass muster with someone else—say his doctor or nurse?"

"I've been thinking about that kind of test, Jack," Stevens said with a nod. "The doctor and nurse wouldn't be very good judges, since they haven't known Powder long. There's a better way. It's a test that we've saved until last. If you pass it, you'll be able to pass as Powder anywhere."

"I'm ready for it," Jack said.

"We're going to allow Powder's girl friend to visit him," Stevens said. "Do you think you could fool Betty Brown?"

"Betty!"

Jack had been so busy that he hadn't figured out the obvious answer to Betty's flight from Tennessee to the

Coast and her reference to her sweetheart hurt in an airplane crash. Powder was Betty's fiancé!

"Don't get excited, Jack," Stevens said. "You've got a job to do. You mustn't let yourself think that because she saved your life once it isn't cricket to spy on her. She may be an enemy of our country and responsible for the deaths of others, even though she saved your life. The stakes we play for are high."

"Are you going to arrest her?" Jack merely asked quietly.

"We haven't got the goods on her yet," Stevens admitted. "Maybe later, after you meet The Head, we'll have our evidence."

It was a difficult task—spying on someone who had saved your life, but Jack did not question the necessity of going on with it.

"What has to be done, has to be done," Jack agreed somberly.

"I knew you'd see it that way, Jack," Stevens said. "Now we'll get ready for this final test. You'll take Powder's place in his room this afternoon and we'll let Betty Brown know that Powder is 'out of danger' and she can visit him."

Stevens went through his plan detail by detail, making sure that Jack understood every phase of the part he was to play. At first Jack would pretend to be asleep. The girl would enter the room. Her first glimpse of the sleeping man would be a test of Jack's general disguise. Then he was to awaken and talk to her. This would test his ability to impersonate Powder's voice and actions. If Jack passed both parts of the test there would be nothing to fear when Jack met The Head, Stevens pointed out.

"What do you mean, 'nothing to fear'?" Jack asked. "The girl will see me only a few minutes, and part of the time I'll be pretending to be asleep. But when I'm with the spy ring, I'll be under observation several days at least."

"Yes," Stevens replied, "but The Head is a man, after all—he may not have studied you as closely as this girl has."

Right after the noon lunch, Powder was placed on a stretcher and moved to another hospital room, while Smilin' Jack donned pajamas and took the place of the spy in the bed.

Jack was slightly nervous.

"Stage fright," he explained to Stevens. "I haven't felt this way since I took part in my high school class play."

"I'm not worried about you, Jack," Stevens replied. "You'll calm down. Remember—everything depends on how completely you fool Betty Brown!"

If only this were some other girl than Betty Brown!

"Come, Jack!" Stevens spoke sternly as he noted the worried expression on Jack's face. "Pull yourself together."

Jack laughed nervously.

"What would she think of me if she discovered I was paying her back for saving my life by causing her arrest?"

"A spy deserves no mercy, Jack," Stevens said. "If she's

guilty, she'll get none."

Jack had made his decision. He wasn't going to back out now. Besides, if Jack didn't go through with the plan, Betty—if she were a spy—might cause the death of thousands of American soldiers and sailors who were fighting for bigger stakes than Smilin' Jack's life. His own life was insignificant in comparison to the importance of succeeding in carrying through this impersonation.

No, Jack wouldn't back out now. He would go on. Everything depended on the success of this masquerade. This was war. Jack's own feelings and all personal considerations were submerged in the national war effort. It was every man's duty to do what was needed to win the victory for United States of America.

Too, what if Betty was not a spy after all? It was hard to imagine her plotting against her own country. If she was not guilty, Jack could perhaps prove her innocence by doing his job well.

"Don't worry about me, Mr. Stevens," Jack assured the FBI chief. "I'll not let you down."

Jack's nervousness vanished. He was calm. His senses were alert. He would do his best to be the precise duplicate of Powder.

"Good boy!" Stevens said, clasping Jack's hand.

The FBI chief left Jack alone in the room. A gentle spring breeze fluttered the curtain at the window.

Faintly at first and then louder, Smilin' Jack heard the click of high-heeled shoes coming down the hospital corridor. The heels stopped in front of the door. Jack heard a hand placed on the door. The knob turned softly.

Betty Brown was entering the hospital room.

Jack's head was on the pillow. He closed his eyes as the faint squeak of hinges told him the door was opening.

This *had* to be good. All the effort he had expended during the preceding eight days would be wasted unless his disguise as Powder Pellet fooled Betty Brown.

The girl stepped into the room. Jack hoped she could not hear the loud thumping of his heart.

Three soft footsteps tapped from the doorway to Smilin' Jack's bed. His eyes remained closed. He dared not risk even a peep at the girl who stood, he was sure, looking down at him.

"Powder!"

Betty's voice came softly, almost in a whisper, but it still was the melodious contralto that Jack had first heard while flying in the fog near Memphis.

The calm expression on Jack's face as he feigned sleep did not change. With trained self-mastery, he kept his eyes closed.

"You poor, poor boy!" Betty spoke gently as she bent over the bed. Her hand touched his forehead. Jack felt the band of the diamond ring, the ring that had been given to her by Powder Pellet.

Why should such a sweet, pleasant, refreshing girl fall for a scoundrel like Powder, and why should she become a traitor to her country— that is, if Betty were actually a spy?

"You were hurt so terribly!" she whispered sympathetically.

Betty had been in the room long enough now to notice anything wrong with the disguise. The first part of the test had been successful, but the most severe part would come in a moment.

Again her hand stroked Jack's brow.

"Why—you're perspiring!" she exclaimed almost aloud. "Your fever must be broken! You're getting well! I'm *so* glad!"

Jack could have told Betty without medical prompting that the perspiration was not the result of a broken fever. But had hospital attendants taken Smilin' Jack's blood pressure at that moment, probably they would have started to feed him oxygen—or maybe they would have run for an air-raid shelter. Jack's blood pressure was—*he* felt—at the exploding point!

The first test had run long enough now. Realizing that he had passed it with flying colors, Smilin' Jack opened his eyes and looked full into the soft blue orbs of Betty Brown at his bedside. He smiled weakly.

"Betty!" he whispered, in perfect imitation of a sick man.

This weak voice, however, was not altogether acting. Jack really felt weak.

"Oh!" Betty exclaimed, half reprimanding herself. "I woke you up."

She returned Jack's smile.

"But I'm glad you did!" Jack said quickly.

He wondered if he had the proper inflection in his voice. Everything depended on whether the girl would see through the disguise or not.

"I'd be angry to learn that you'd been here and I hadn't seen you," he went on.

"This is the first chance I've had to visit you, Powder," Betty explained. "They wouldn't let me in before—they said you were hurt too badly. But you seem normal again. You're getting well, aren't you?"

"I had a bad shock," Jack said. "The doctor was afraid visitors might run up my blood pressure."

As if Jack's blood pressure was low right now!

Betty pulled a chair up to the side of the bed and sat down. She glanced anxiously toward the door.

"A message came for you today, Powder," she said. "I opened it—I thought you wouldn't mind."

Jack's heart was thumping like a bass drum. Would Betty incriminate herself by what she was about to tell him?

"That's all right," Jack said. "Wh-what did it say?"

"It was from The Head," Betty said.

She *was* incriminating herself—she must be involved personally.

"About the meeting?" Jack asked, quietly.

"Yes, Powder," Betty whispered. "Since your plane was cracked up, you won't have to fly to meet him. He'll send Jim in a seaplane to meet you on the shore directly west of Belvu. Will you be ready to make the flight in another week?"

"I could leave now," Jack said, "but the doctor says I'll have to stick around a little while."

"Good. I'll wire father and he'll tell The Head."

So Betty's father was in on it too. That placed Betty in this ring deeper than ever.

"I won't see you again, Powder," Betty said. "I'm leaving tonight. But after your job is done, we'll see each other again."

"Sure!"

Jack gulped, realizing that the next time he saw Betty Brown might be at her trial as a spy against the United States.

Betty clasped Jack's hand.

"Now let's talk about something else besides business," she said.

"Sure!" Jack exclaimed. "Nothing would suit me better —right now."

But at that moment the door opened again and a nurse appeared.

"I'm so sorry, Miss Brown," the nurse said. "But your time is up. You'll have to leave now. Doctor's orders."

"Not even another minute?"

The nurse shook her head.

"His condition still isn't quite satisfactory for a long visit," the nurse said.

"Oh, well!"

Leaning forward Betty planted a kiss on Jack's cheek, and then turned away. She paused at the door to look back again at Jack with a good-bye smile.

"I'll be seeing you!" she said.

"Yes," Jack answered, as Betty disappeared through the door. "We'll see each other again, never fear."

The door closed softly behind the girl. The nurse nodded at Jack and left the room.

Jack raised up in the bed. He had passed a test which he almost hoped he would not pass. Nothing stood in his way—there was nothing to prevent his "repaying" Betty for saving his life by exposing her as a spy: an extremely distasteful duty, but still his duty.

As Stevens came from the next room through a connecting door, Jack swung his feet out of bed.

"Great work, Jack!" the FBI operative exclaimed. "You were perfect! I watched the whole thing through the one-way glass panel and you handled the situation like an old trouper! Even Powder's mother would have been fooled by the act you put on. And we learned some things from it, too!"

"Thanks," Smilin' Jack said drily. "Are—are you going to arrest her?"

"Not right away," Stevens said. "Her arrest might tip off The Head that we're onto his plans. Later, perhaps we may."

Tossing his dressing gown over his broad shoulders, Jack hurried into his own room where he quickly dressed. Attendants wheeled the real Powder back into the room Jack had just vacated.

"Powder's about well enough to be taken to a detention camp," Stevens said. "But we'll hold him here until you've studied him awhile longer. Then you can go to Belvu to keep Powder's rendezvous with this seaplane."

"I'm ready to go any time," Jack said.

The telephone extension in Jack's room rang. Stevens picked up the receiver:

"Yes—yes, this is Stevens.—Yes.—Okay."

The FBI man hung up the receiver. His face was grave as he turned to Jack.

"We were having Betty Brown followed," he said. "But our shadow got caught in a traffic jam on the way to the airport. When he got to the flying field she was gone."

"Well?"

"What if she saw through your disguise and didn't let on?" Stevens asked pointedly. "Perhaps she's gone to warn other members of the ring. If she has, your life isn't worth a plugged nickel!"

"Whew!" Jack exclaimed.

He hadn't thought of this obvious possibility. He had been patting himself on the back as having completely fooled Betty. But she might have been masquerading too. A clever spy wouldn't reveal everything that passed through her mind.

"Are you still willing to take the chance, Jack?" Stevens asked, fixing his gimlet eyes on the aviator.

The assignment, perilous enough without the added complication, afforded new dangers now. There was no way of knowing how much Betty Brown had guessed during her interview with Jack in the hospital. There was a possibility that she had guessed nothing, and an equal

chance that she had seen completely through Jack's disguise. But the first chance offered an opportunity to trap
the spy ring. It was worth taking.

"I'm no quitter!" Smilin' Jack said firmly.

CHAPTER FOUR

THE KISS OF DEATH

The following days passed slowly, but at last the zero hour arrived. It was time for Smilin' Jack's rendezvous with the seaplane at Belvu.

Stevens issued last minute instructions to Jack as he took him by car to the little coastal town in southern California.

"Your trip may take you into neutral countries of South America," he said. "As you know, some of the South American countries are not at war with the Axis and your conduct in those nations must be guided accordingly. You'll be entirely on your own. You must act on your own initiative in those lands, for the United States has no legal power to endorse your actions outside of its national boundaries."

"I understand," Jack acknowledged. "If I'm caught, I can expect no aid from Uncle Sam."

"And you must keep in mind that the entire success or failure of this mission depends on you. If you fail, it may cost the lives of many boys overseas. If you succeed, valuable lives will be saved."

"I don't intend to fail."

"You *must not* fail," Stevens said with determination. "I believe in you, Jack. Nothing must stop you from

53

learning the set-up operated by The Head so we can
bring his gang to justice. Once you have landed him, the
whole ring will be crushed. That's worth a severe defeat
on the battlefield for the enemy."

Jack nodded as he realized that there was an implica-
tion that if *he* were defeated, it would mean a defeat for
the United States. This was a desperate game and the
stakes were high. One man's life meant nothing in the
total score. Jack could not hold his own life highly—nor
must he hesitate even though it placed a woman, the
woman who had saved his life, behind prison bars.

Stevens let Jack out of the car on the outskirts of Belvu.
As Jack sauntered through the torrid little village, he
could not get over the feeling that he was being watched.
Nerves, he supposed.

He passed through the town and went to the beach
where the sea lashed a rocky shore. A small cove a couple
of miles north of the town seemed to be the logical place
for the seaplane to land. Just before dusk Jack arrived
at the spot. Seating himself on a rock he watched the sun
sink into the western ocean. Dusk faded into twilight
and twilight into night. Jack waited, listening to the roar
of the waves.

Then, faintly above the sound of the beating surf,
Smilin' Jack heard the familiar hum of an airplane motor.
The seaplane was coming!

Jack was on his feet, straining his eyes toward the sea.
Then he caught a glimpse of the plane's lights as it hit
the surf and taxied toward the shore.

The Plane Hit the Surf and Taxied Toward Shore

The pilot—Jim, Betty said his name was—apparently was thoroughly familiar with every inch of the coastline, for he avoided the treacherous rocks expertly and brought his plane to rest on the edge of the beach.

Tensely and cautiously, Smilin' Jack made his way forward to where the plane idled its motors. Here was another test of his disguise that might unexpectedly result in discovery. Jack could never be sure of continuing success in his impersonation of Powder. Besides, Betty might have suspected something at the hospital and the pilot might have orders to finish Jack off, instead of picking him up.

A gruff voice sounded from the plane. "Hold it!"

Jack halted in his tracks. A flashlight gleamed in the cockpit and its beam fastened itself on Jack.

"That you, Powder?" the voice called.

"Yeah!" Jack answered huskily—the strain was beginning to tell on him.

The flashlight traveled from Jack's head to his shoes while the pilot looked him over.

"Uh-huh!" came the voice. "No mistakin' that handsome face, you old rascal. Heard you cracked up."

"Not much—guess I was lucky," Jack said. "It kept me in the hospital awhile, but doc said it was mostly shock."

"Did you get rid of everything before you crashed?" the pilot asked.

"Sure—Jim—" Jack decided to risk the name; and when there was no reaction he felt safer. "—Think I was born yesterday?"

"Come on over here," Jim ordered.

The voice was a little gruffer. Had Jack made a miscue? Maybe this man wasn't Jim.

With leaden feet Jack moved toward the flashlight.

"Far enough!" the pilot commanded as Jack reached the side of the seaplane. "Lemme see your left hand."

Smilin' Jack almost whistled his sigh of relief. He was certainly glad now that he had undergone the painful branding of the symbol on his hand: the secret mark of the spy ring!

Jack thrust his left-palm into the rays of the flashlight. The pilot gave it a cursory inspection and nodded.

"Yeah. That's okay. I just wanted to make sure—The Head's orders, you know, old man."

"Sure, Jim. I understand." Jack felt much relieved.

"We can't take any chances nowadays," Jim said. "It ain't like the old days when all we did was shanghai bums for Death Rock."

The reference went over Jack's head, and Jack grunted noncommitally.

"Nope. We can't take chances."

"All right, toss away that foul-smellin' cigar—same old brand, I see—an' jump in. We've got a lot of flyin' to do," the pilot said.

As Jack boarded the seaplane he saw Jim putting away a forty-five automatic. That cannon had been trained on Jack during the first interview. One false move and it would have ended his part in the American war effort. Jack was more than thankful for the long hours he had spent in learning well how to impersonate the man known as Powder.

After holstering the automatic, Jim turned to his passenger.

"We're gonna take it slow and easy," he announced. "The Head said you'd probably be so weak from the hospital that you couldn't stand makin' this trip in one jump. Anyhow, we've got to do most of our flyin' at night to avoid patrol planes. We'll stop at the usual hide-outs in Mexico and South America, an' meet The Head at sea in about three days."

"It ought to be a nice, pleasant trip," Jack said.

Jim laughed.

"Same ol' Powder—always cool, never afraid of nuttin'. But don't worry. Old Jimmy can get us past Panama without no trouble."

Getting "past Panama" was an item Jack hadn't thought of. Uncle Sam maintained a constant patrol of fighter planes in the vicinity of the Canal Zone. They were almost certain to be stopped unless they wanted to risk a little machine-gunning from faster and better planes.

Jim gunned the motor and the seaplane began taxiing out to sea.

Through the night the seaplane flew. Hour after hour passed without incident. The noise of the motor dinned in Jack's ears until at last the first streaks of dawn appeared in the east. Then the airplane settled down along the coast of Mexico.

Among the trees was a large building, constructed of logs and carefully camouflaged. The building was filled with drums of oil. This was a secret seaplane and submarine base maintained by Fifth Columnists!

Jack made a mental note of the landmarks around the place. Later, if he got through his trip safely, the information would be communicated to American authorities who would see that the place was put out of operation.

The most dangerous part of the trip lay ahead. The flying through the area near the Panama Canal would mean constant peril. Patrols, warships, listening devices of all kinds could detect the approach of any aircraft— and all unidentified planes were warded off, by force if necessary.

But Jim seemed not to worry about the future. As the plane took off at dusk on the second leg of its southward flight, Jack noticed that Jim was climbing steadily.

At eighteen thousand feet, Jim signaled for Jack to begin using oxygen. The plane went still higher. It passed the twenty-thousand-foot level and continued to climb. Finally it leveled off at twenty-five thousand feet.

As nearly as Jack was able to determine his position, the plane was still about one hundred and fifty miles north of the Panama Canal when it reached its top level. But listening devices can easily detect planes that far away. Posts at the canal already were aware of the approach of the seaplane! Air-raid alarms were sounding and interceptor pilots were scrambling into their planes.

Jack was as sure of these preparations as if he were

taking part in them!

Gunners were manning anti-aircraft cannon. The Canal Zone defenders were on the alert. No doubt every military establishment in the zone knew that "an unidentified aircraft" was flying southward toward the lifeline of the United States Navy.

Jim had opened the throttle wide—the plane was traveling at least 300 miles an hour. At this speed, the seaplane would pass the Canal in about thirty minutes—not a long time, but time enough for interceptor planes to get high into the air.

Jim flipped off his lights now and flew in total darkness, still keeping his altitude.

Jack watched below. As the moon peeped out from behind a cloud, he caught a glimpse of the silvery ribbon of the Panama Canal cutting from southwest to northeast across the isthmus. No planes were visible yet, but they probably were in the sky, flying dark to intercept the strange aircraft.

A searchlight stabbed into the sky. Then another! There seemed to be a line of bars of light blocking the path of the seaplane. To fly into one of these beams meant death from anti-aircraft guns below.

Toward this network of destruction, the seaplane carrying Smilin' Jack flew at top speed.

Suddenly Jim leaned forward and cut the engine. Silence closed in over the plane.

The searchlights stabbed frantically into the sky, seeking to find the silent intruder. Jack's heart bounced up into his throat as those long silvery arms wove closer and closer to the seaplane.

Above the whisper of the seaplane's propeller, Jack heard the roar of fighter planes below, trying to locate the seaplane. But Jim was still flying at high altitude and his craft was only a tiny, almost invisible speck in the sky.

Jim's speed and altitude would enable him to glide for miles, silent as an arrow.

In a few minutes the seaplane had dodged through the bars of light. Jim started the motor and the seaplane raced for safety over the South American republic of Colombia.

The most dangerous leg of the journey had been completed.

"Nice work, Jim!" Smilin' Jack muttered as Powder would have said it.

But his words were drowned out by the roar of the seaplane's motors. Jim never heard the words, nor did he know that he had done Uncle Sam a great service by dodging the air defenses of the Panama Canal. It might have been better for the enemy spies to have had a less able pilot than Jim that night.

At dawn the seaplane settled down along the coast of the South American nation where another enemy base was located. Smilin' Jack made a second mental note of the location which would aid in the final round-up of enemy spies. This series of Axis bases from California to the Pacific coast of South America was undoubtedly designed to serve for more than underground railway stations for spies.

Submarines could be refueled there, for instance—enemy subs that were prowling the seas to sink merchantmen carrying supplies to the forces of the United Nations.

Jack also learned some useful facts about Jim. The pilot, he learned, was one of those unscrupulous, worthless airmen who sell their services to smuggle contraband merchandise and fly dope into the United States in peacetime.

No respectable aviation company would have hired a man of Jim's type, and his record barred him from Army service. With flying as Jim's only art, he had sold himself to The Head—another peacetime smuggler as well as an international Axis spy—for a job. Jim had been willing to betray his native country for a few dollars that he might never have a chance to spend.

After eating and resting at the coastal base, the plane took off in daylight, flying west this time over the waters of the Pacific.

Late in the day a small yacht was sighted. Jim cut his speed and circled the ship, which seemed to be at anchor. Then he signaled for Jack to buckle his safety belt for a landing.

The seaplane glided toward the waves. It struck the rough surf and taxied through the waves toward the ship.

A crane on the deck lowered a hook, which Jim fastened to a ring just behind the motor. Slowly the seaplane and its two passengers were lifted from the water and placed on the deck.

Jim turned to Jack and grinned.

"Well, Powder," he said. "We made it!"

"Good enough!" said Jack, not forgetting to use Powder's tone of voice and inflection. "Part of the way I had my doubts."

"Aw, it was easy!" Jim said in self-deprecation.

The pilot hopped to the deck and Jack followed him. A ship's officer was hurrying toward them as Jack hit the deck.

"Hello, Powder!" the officer greeted. "The Head is expecting you, but he sent word that he won't be able to see you until tomorrow."

"Okay," Jack said. "I'm pretty tired anyhow."

Jack was thankful for a chance to rest before subjecting his disguise to another test. The following day he would be refreshed and ready to pose as Powder before The Head, astute and shrewd chief of the espionage ring.

Stretching his muscles, wearily, Jack turned to the officer.

"Where's my cabin, sir? I'd like to turn in."

"I'll show you," the officer said. "It's No. X-13. Just follow me."

The officer led him to a gangway leading to the lower deck. Before he reached the steps, a small figure pushed up from below and rushed past the officer toward Smilin' Jack.

"Powder!" a girl's voice screamed in delighted surprise.

The shrill cry was followed by happy laughter as the figure collided with Jack. He felt small arms twine about his neck and a kiss planted on his cheek. He caught the fragrance of a familiar perfume that somehow reminded him of the hospital at Valley Ridge.

The girl stood back, surveying Jack.

"Powder!" she exclaimed. "It's so good to see you again!"

At last Jack knew the voice as the girl spoke in her normal tone. He saw her familiar face as she stood away from him.

Betty Brown was on the yacht!

"Betty!" Jack said, beaming with happiness that was not altogether feigned. "So you beat me here!"

"I had a week's leeway, Jack!" she explained. "I would be a pretty poor flier if I couldn't have made it with such a head start. But the way I got held up at the Panama Canal made me think I'd never get here."

"How *did* you get through?" Jack asked.

"Why, father did it, of course!" Betty exclaimed, almost as though "Powder" should have known that without asking.

Jack would like to know more about Betty's father. Who was he? How did he manage to smuggle Betty in a strange plane past the Panama Canal?

"Well, Powder," Betty said. "Don't just stand there staring at me!"

"Huh?" Jack said, jarred out of his thoughts.

"I meant, aren't you going to kiss me?"

"Ah—"

Jack hesitated.

"Powder!" the girl's voice rang out complainingly.

"Your Cabin Is X-13," the Officer Said

"Aren't you glad to see me? You act so strange—so cool!"

If he was not careful, this girl would be suspicious enough to see through the disguise. Jack couldn't let himself fail now. He had to act just as Powder might have acted. He had to behave as though he were in love with Betty Brown, even though she might be a deadly enemy.

Everything depended on Jack now: he couldn't afford to miss any bets. He had to kiss her.

Impelled by necessity but with considerable inward reluctance, Smilin' Jack pulled Betty toward him. He took her in his arms and delivered what seemed to him to be a kiss of death.

Certainly it was a fake caress—a Judas kiss!

Betty stood back.

"For a minute I thought you didn't care," she said, laughing. "Well, I suppose you're tired out from your long trip. Oh, I almost forgot, Powder, you're just out of the hospital. How selfish of me to keep you from getting some rest!"

"I didn't mind," Jack said.

The strange part about it was that he wouldn't have minded the kiss under ordinary circumstances, but he did mind the circumstance that it was not Smilin' Jack but Powder whom Betty thought she had kissed.

"I'll show you to your stateroom now, sir," the officer spoke.

"If you'll excuse me, then—"

"Of course, Powder," Betty said. "I'll see you later."

Jack followed the officer below deck. He was shown to a small stateroom numbered X-13.

"I hope you're not superstitious, Powder," the officer said, glancing at the number significantly.

"Well," Jack said, "if I were, I probably couldn't do anything about it."

"That's right," the officer agreed. "The Head ordered me to assign you to this cabin."

The Head had a nice way of making his guests feel comfortable, apparently. Glancing up the corridor, Jack saw that *all* of the cabins were numbered thirteen! They were distinguished one from another only by the letter of the alphabet which preceded the number.

Well, it looked as though members of this particular spy ring were not a superstitious lot.

CHAPTER FIVE

THE HEAD AND THE CLAW

Smilin' Jack did not see Betty at breakfast the next morning. In fact, except for one or two members of the crew, he was alone at breakfast.

"Not much adoin' here in the mornin'," the steward told Jack. "Like the owls, we live mostly at night."

"Owls or wolves?" Jack asked, in a manner that the steward did not fully grasp. "Wolves roam at night, too."

"Ha, ha! Very good, sir!" the steward said with a laugh. "Ah, yes—*wolves.*"

After breakfast, Jack walked the deck. So far his trip had been productive and his disguise had been impenetrable. No one seemed to suspect that he was anyone but Powder—and Powder apparently held a position high up in the ring.

Jim, who had flown Jack from the United States, had certainly not seemed in the least uneasy during the brief stops at enemy bases. Jack, in fact, had been able to make observations at the bases that would lead to their capture or destruction as soon as he was able to communicate with Mr. Stevens.

What big plans were afoot, Jack wondered, that had caused this meeting at sea? After Jack had learned these plans, he could begin preparations to escape to the mainland and contact American officials at some South American consulate. After that the whole spy ring could be smashed.

Yet there remained one unpleasantly distasteful aspect of the whole business. What about Betty Brown? How had she gotten mixed up in this band of international criminals? Had she been brought into its circle by Powder, or had she been a member before her acquaintance with him? To look at her, one would never suspect her of even the most casual associaiton with such a man as Powder.

When the spy ring was rounded up, Betty would be arrested along with the others. No matter how innocent she might look, if she were guilty she would deserve punishment for being a traitor to her country.

Traitor! The word seemed wholly foreign and outlandish when applied to Betty.

"She simply can't be a spy!" Jack resolved, rather foolishly--since all evidence pointed to her as one of the gang.

Jack had been so busy thinking that the soft-footed steward's approach was unnoticed. When he saw the man at his side, Jack gave a start.

"The Head sends his compliments and asks you to come to his cabin," the steward announced.

"Thanks, steward."

First tossing away his cigar—the black, foul-smelling brand that Powder preferred—Jack obeyed orders.

Jack felt no particular fears as he entered the luxuriously

furnished cabin that served as The Head's quarters. Jack already was confident that his disguise would fool the spy chief. His chief concern was that he would be asked something he could not answer. But Jack consoled himself with the reminder of Agent Stevens to the effect that men of Powder's caliber rarely discussed their past.

Jack's eyes became accustomed to the darkened room as he entered the door and came face to face with the man known as The Head. He was almost visibly startled by the weird appearance of the notorious international spy.

Jack had no idea what sort of looking man The Head would be, but he had expected something quite different from what he saw.

No canny cleverness appeared in the face; there was no importance or dignity in the features. The face was neither intellectual nor distinguished. The Head was uncommonly insignificant—to look at. He was an absurdly tiny man —completely bald, with large, Oriental eyes, and a weak, pusillanimous mouth. As he sat behind a large, highly polished desk he looked like a mere toad of a man. The drooping eyelids concealed a languorous stare.

"Did you send for me—Chief?" Jack asked, in Powder's inflection.

"Yes, Powder!"

The weak voice seemed insultingly intoned, until Jack realized that this was the man's natural way of speaking. He apparently looked upon other human beings with the condescension that a whale might feel for a mollusk, his diminutive stature notwithstanding.

"I am very glad to see you," The Head began in a voice that seemed to say that he would have been just as happy if Jack were never seen by anyone again. "Your accident did not seem to hurt you seriously. You're looking better than I ever saw you before."

A chill ran up Smilin' Jack's spine—did The Head already suspect the masquerade?

"Thanks, Chief. They fed me well at the hospital."

Outwardly Smilin' Jack gave not sign of his uneasiness.

"And of course Betty was there to see you often!"

Jack was about to answer when he noted a tiny twist to The Head's mouth. The spy was trying to trap him! The spy knew that Betty had *not* been permitted to see Powder often.

"Well, the doctor wouldn't let her in to see me very much, Chief," Jack said. "Afraid it might run up my blood pressure."

The Head smiled, toying with a sharp letter opener. At last he chuckled, mirthlessly, and touched a button on his desk. A door opened at the side of the cabin and through it came a huge, waddling bulk of a man.

The newcomer was even more grotesque than the shriveled dwarf-like man known as The Head. Naked to the waist, he was, so to speak, modeled on gorilla lines. His skull was bald, like The Head's, but its shape was like the nose of a bullet. His beetle brows were surmounted by black, scowling grooves of flesh. His nose was bashed to one side as though it had been forced to follow the twisted lines of his mouth.

"It is well that you answered truthfully, Powder," The Head said. "I was afraid that some of your papers might have fallen into the hands of American counter-espionage agents and that you were a disguised impostor sent here to learn some damaging details of our organization. For that reason I had your old friend The Claw in the next room, ready to use his little hook—"

The Claw laughed derisively, and raised his right arm. Instead of a hand, Jack saw an ugly metal hook fastened to the stump of his amputated lower arm.

"Glad to see you again, Claw," Jack said, forcing a smile —as he hoped Powder would have smiled.

"Ugh!" The Claw grunted non-committally.

"He is still unfriendly toward everyone but me, Powder," The Head remarked with a certain smugness. "It is somewhat of a disappointment to him that he did not get to sink his claw into you."

Smilin' Jack laughed in order to conceal the shudder he felt.

"Well," The Head continued, "I suppose we'd better get down to business. Your job, as you may have expected, has to do with flying."

"I thought so." Jack nodded. "Seemed likely, anyhow."

"Have you ever flown one of the new model patrol bombers the American navy uses in the Pacific?" came the question.

"Why, no—those ships are pretty well-guarded secrets!"

"They won't be for long," The Head said knowingly. "But I see no reason why you couldn't fly one—you could

The Claw Raised His Right Arm

familiarize yourself with the controls in a short time. After that, flying a patrol bomber is like flying any other kind of craft."

"Yes," Jack said. "I could fly one, I suppose."

"I am stealing one of the patrol bombers," The Head announced. "Two of my agents in the American navy arranged to be on one of the bombers during a test flight. They 'disappeared' last night, and by spreading some oil on the ocean and planting some pieces of wreckage they should have fooled the navy into thinking they crashed at sea. Instead, they simply dumped other members of the crew overboard—so the bomber now is flying here to meet me. You are to fly it on to one of the Japanese-held islands."

The boldness of The Head's plan left Smilin' Jack almost stunned. Actually to steal a patrol bomber from under Uncle Sam's nose! But The Head wouldn't get away with it: already Uncle Sam was "in the know," for Jack was acting for Uncle Sam. Once Jack was at the controls, he could fly back to the mainland—

"The Claw will be your companion on the trip, Powder," The Head added with an evil smile. "Now, I know you are very anxious to talk to Betty. She is on the forward deck. Good morning—Powder!"

Jack was not altogether sure of his success as he emerged from his conference with The Head. The master spy either was unduly cautious or he suspected something. Smilin' Jack only hoped he would have an opportunity to communicate with Stevens before The Head trapped him and revealed that he was indeed not Powder—but a trusted agent carrying out a mission for the U. S. A.

Betty was waiting for Jack—she ran to meet him as the aviator left the cabin.

"I was wondering how long you were going to talk business with Mr. Ghindi," Betty said.

Mr. Ghindi—that probably was The Head's name. Jack made a mental note of it for future reference.

"Pretty *bad* business, Betty." Jack spoke slowly. He was on thin ice and he watched Betty's eyes as he spoke. "Don't you sometimes wish you'd taken up *another*—kind of business?"

"Why, Powder!" Betty laughed. "I think it's the most fascinating business in the world. But I guess it's in my blood. My father has been in this business in South America for fifteen years."

The girl was absolutely sincere: she enjoyed being a spy! She came from a *family* of international spies. Jack could hardly credit his own ears.

"Well, Powder," Betty said, taking Jack's arm. "Here we are on my yacht in the middle of the Pacific—"

So it was Betty's yacht!

"—just as we planned," she finished warmly.

"Yes," Jack said, wondering what the girl was driving at. "Just as we planned."

"Shall we go ahead with the schedule today, or later?"

"Right now!" Jack said.

"Now? The same old Powder! Always impetuous! But I couldn't get ready before afternoon. A girl can't get married like she'd buy a new dress, even though we planned this elopement."

Marriage! Elopement!

It suddenly dawned on Jack what Betty had been talking about. She and Powder had planned on being married during this meeting with The Head—combining business with romance. What kind of cold-blooded, heartless creature was this daredevil girl, mixing "love" with betrayal of her native land.

Betty was soon busy formulating a program. They could be married during the afternoon with the captain officiating and Mr. Ghindi as best man. The stewardess could be matron of honor. Jack's head spun at the swiftness with which events were following one another in his new role.

"Mr. Ghindi said that there may be submarines in these waters and we're only to send one message apiece," Betty went on.

A message! That was the answer. If Jack could send a message to Stevens he might get United States naval planes here in time to foil the theft of the patrol bomber.

"Let's send the messages now!" Jack suggested. "Then we won't have anything to think about after the ceremony."

"Oh, Powder! I've never seen you so flustered! But maybe it would be a good idea. Who are *you* going to tell?"

"Well," Jack said slowly, "I've an old friend back in Valley Ridge—Stevens—I guess he ought to know."

"All right. I'll send mine to father and you let your friend know."

Jack hoped that he could make Stevens understand so Stevens would get the navy on the job before the wedding ceremony could take place.

"Come on," Jack said. "Where's the radio room?"

"Oh, I'm so *thrilled!*" Betty said, excitedly, as she led the way to the top deck.

Jack quickly collected his thoughts. He would have to tell Stevens that the PB craft—patrol bomber—was being stolen and where to find it. Jack didn't know their latitude and longitude, but he did know they were somewhere near Peru. He would have to send a message that would say one thing but *mean* something else. He could use the letters PB as initials for Stevens name! P. B. Stevens! That would warn Stevens right away to be on the alert.

Betty led the way into the radio room.

"What are you going to say, Powder?" she asked, with a natural feminine curiosity.

"Oh, something to kid him along," Jack said.

First picking up paper and pencil, he began to write slowly, making sure he was saying two things at once. At last he finished and handed the message to Betty, who read:

"'P. B. Stevens, 444 East Twelfth Street, Valley Ridge, California. Perfect elopement remedies unsoundness. Smile! And check—it's not lost but stolen love. Thief is Betty Brown in the middle of Pacific. Powder!'"

Betty blinked, her forehead in furrows. "It isn't very coherent, but maybe he'll understand it. Why don't you just say: 'Eloped with Betty'?"

"He's a newspaper man," Jack said. "That first sentence is written headline style because he probably wouldn't understand any other kind of lingo."

"I guess it is sort of clever," Betty conceded dubiously. "You go ahead and write one for my father while I hunt up the captain. He'll have to okay the messages— it's some sort of war regulation Mr. Ghindi explained to me."

As Betty left, Jack checked an impulse to overpower the radio operator and send a message himself. But the odds were against him. The radio operator was armed and Jack could hardly take him by surprise.

That cryptic message to Stevens *had* to get through.

"Couldn't you start sending this now—to save time?" Jack asked the operator.

The radio officer turned to Jack and picked up the message.

"Did The Head see this?" he asked.

"No—" Jack began.

"But I'll be pleased to read it now," came a sarcastic voice from behind Jack.

Jack whirled to come face to face with the little man, who extended a tiny arm and jerked the paper from the radio operator's hand.

"I was telling a chum about Betty and me getting married," Jack explained. "He's the kind of screwball who'll

Betty Led the Way to the Radio Room

get a wallop out of that scrambled radiogram."

The Head did not reply. His right hand went inside his coat and an automatic appeared from a shoulder holster. With the weapon pointed at Jack, The Head's lips parted in an evil grin.

"Even your innermost thoughts could not be hidden from me, Powder," he said. "I have suspected you since you first came aboard. Somehow you did not act altogether like the real Powder—perhaps it was your manner, or it may have been that you did not look *dissipated* enough."

Another shadow blacked out the door. It was The Claw coming into the room. His ugly hook was lifted and there was a grin of evil anticipation on his vicious face.

"Shall I throw him to the sharks, Chief?" he asked eagerly.

The Head holstered his pistol.

"Not yet," he said. "I want to read this interesting message addressed to 'P.B. Stevens.' 'P.B.' could not possibly refer to *patrol bomber,* could it, Powder?"

Smilin' Jack was silent. A thousand times as he had rehearsed his role as Powder, he had foreseen the possibility of being discovered as a masquerader. He had wondered if he would be afraid. He was angry at being in the power of such an insignificant little scoundrel.

Outwardly Jack was calm, composed, waiting for a chance.

The dwarfed man was not giving Jack a chance, however.

"You needn't tell me, Powder," he went on. "I can guess. Now that first sentence intrigues me: *'Perfect elopement remedies unsoundness.'* At first glance I'd say it was nonsense, but isn't it a coincidence that the initials of those four words are P-E-R-U, *Peru,* the country nearest our location in the Pacific!"

Jack compressed his lips tightly. The Head was no dunce—he was doing a good job of deciphering the message.

"And there are other acrobatics with words in this odd message. For instance: *'Smile'!* What does that mean? It might not be intended to be set off by itself. Perhaps it is part of the next sentence: *'Smile and check.'* Could that mean something?"

To Jack it meant something, but to The Head it did not. To Jack it was his own name, "Smilin' Jack," as closely as he could have said it in a message likely to be censored. Stevens undoubtedly would have read it "Smilin' Jack" as he deciphered it.

"The meaning escapes me," The Head went on. "I must congratulate you for making part of the message undecipherable. But the rest is quite clear: *'It's not lost but stolen.'* Referring to the plane, not to 'love'' as you wrote in the message. *'Thief is Betty Brown in middle of Pacific.'* That is redundant. You've already told your friend you were off Peru and it is nonsensical to incriminate Betty Brown. I resent your attributing my feats to others. But perhaps you wanted to tell your friend that Betty Brown's yacht was involved. Yes, that is probably what you meant, although I did not know that you had learned the yacht belonged to her. Powder knew this, but you didn't. You see, I know you are not really Powder."

Jack lunged forward, but his charge toward The Head was checked sharply by a pressure in his shoulder. The Claw had fastened his hook into Jack's clothing and the point was pressing against Jack's skin.

"Lock him in the hold, Claw," The Head ordered. "We'll keep him there until we reach the next coral reef. Then we'll plant him on it—to die!"

"Chee, Boss! I could do it much better!"

"Much messier, too, no doubt! No, Claw. Do as I say, and do it now!"

Jack was marched through the door. As he emerged on deck he saw Betty running toward him.

"Powder!" she cried.

The Head stepped between Jack and Betty.

"It is fortunate for you, Miss Brown, that Powder did not send that message," he said. "It wasn't the kind of message you thought it was."

"You—you mean Powder's a—a spy?" Betty stammered.

"The message would have given the enemy a great deal of valuable information, Miss Brown," The Head said, glancing swiftly from under lowered eyelids at Jack.

"I—I can't believe it!" came the girl's low, troubled sob.

"March!" The Claw ordered, pricking Jack's shoulder

with the hook.

Jack stumbled toward the gangway. It was harder than ever for him to believe that Betty was a member of this unprincipled band of plotters and killers.

CHAPTER SIX

PUZZLING EVIDENCE

With The Claw's sharp hook menacing Jack at every step, the American aviator walked down a narrow, ladder-like stairway to the dark and smelly hold of the yacht.

Here the tropical heat, abetted by the boilers in the engine room, made the atmosphere stifling and stagnant.

Sometimes pushing and sometimes prodding, The Claw hurried Jack forward of the engine room to a small room fitted with a barred door.

"De brig," The Claw announced, catching Jack's shoulder with his hook and holding him while he removed some keys from his pocket with his left hand.

The lock turned and the door swung open on rusty hinges.

"Nuttin' like a cell wit' hot an' cold runnin' rats," The Claw chortled. "Take it easy, Powder. Don't try t' jerk away: dis claw ain't made of rubber."

With that, The Claw pushed Jack into the cell. Still holding his prisoner to prevent a sudden break, the bullet-headed giant examined the room to make sure there were no bits of iron or wood that could be fashioned into crude weapons or tools of escape.

Assuring himself that the only objects in the room were a mattress for a bed and a battered chair, The Claw flung Jack to the floor and made his exit. He locked the cell door and removed the key. Then he paused for a moment to gloat over the prisoner.

"Lockin' you up ain't my way of handlin' you," The Claw said with a snarling laugh. "You're lucky. I could fix you up with my claw, but The Head is a pig. He wants to have all de fun."

Smilin' Jack sat in the chair and rubbed his shoulder where the hook had gouged his flesh. He heard The Claw's footsteps retreat down the passage to the ladder leading to the upper deck.

Alone, Jack peeled off his coat and unfastened his tie and collar. It was suffocatingly hot and this was only the beginning. Jack did not doubt that The Head planned to put him ashore on some coral reef, without food or water. If that wasn't The Head's plan, something worse was in store.

"I've got to escape somehow," Jack vowed.

Not only was his own life at stake, but the information he had gained had to be communicated to American authorities on the mainland.

Jack began a survey of his surroundings. The one porthole in the cell was barred and bolted shut—no chance to escape from that. The bulkhead was strong.

He tried the door. It rattled, but it was solid. The lock was large but Jack didn't have anything to use to pick it. There wasn't a loose bit of metal in the cell and Jack had nothing of that kind on his person.

Escape seemed absolutely impossible.

Jack sat down on the dirty mattress to consider his plight. He might try to overpower his jailer when the next meal was served. But even if he did, what chance would he then have to escape from the ship? The yacht probably was miles from land.

A rat scratched in one corner of the cell. The Claw had not understated his suggestion that Jack would have rodent companionship in his prison. There was another scratching noise—

Jack turned his head. The sound seemed to come from above. Were the rats crawling on the ceiling, too?

A grill was overhead. The noise came from there— the opening from the ventilator!

"Da-da-de-dee!"

No rat made that sound.

"Powder! Can you hear me?"

Betty was calling Jack through the ventilator.

"Betty!" Jack called softly. "Yes, I can hear you—"

"Lucky thing I know more about this ship than they do. What are they doing to you?"

Jack hesitated. How far did he dare to trust Betty? She was a trusted member of this spy ring. Yet—she might not be—perhaps she could help.

"Betty," Jack asked. "How deeply are you mixed up in Mr. Ghindi's—The Head's business?"

"Why, you know as well as I, Powder. You know he's been associated with my father for years—just as you have—"

Betty's father, then, was the boss of the ring and The

The Claw Locked the Door and Took the Key

Head was his associate.

Betty had broken off suddenly in her reply to Jack. Now her voice came again through the ventilator, but she was not speaking to Jack.

"I was trying to find out, Mr. Ghindi, just why you have locked up my fiancé." The Head had arrived on the scene.

"That is quite easy to explain, Miss Brown," replied the Head's voice. "Your fiancé was a spy. He was preparing to turn over your father's secrets to a friend on the mainland. The message he wrote, presumably telling his friend of your elopement, was in code—"

"Powder!" Betty's voice rang through the ventilator. "I can't believe it. Tell me the truth!"

Jack was silent, thinking. If Betty's father were one of the chiefs of this spy ring, then Betty was in it too.

"I thought there was something fishy about that radiogram!" Betty said. "You *are* a spy! And to think I would have married you!"

An object rattled down the ventilator and dropped to Jack's feet on the floor. Jack picked it up. It was the diamond ring.

Without replying to the girl, Jack dropped the ring into his pocket. He heard her leave the ventilator in company with The Head, who apparently had overheard her conversation with Jack and had interrupted it. Betty Brown, the girl with the soft contralto voice, was a Mata Hari unmasked—a woman no man loyal to his country should ever trust.

While Jack was eating his noon meal, which a sailor had brought to the brig, the engine stopped. The rattle of anchor chains sounded at the bow. Something was afoot.

Pushing his plate aside, Jack stood up and peered from the porthole. On this side of the ship was only the rolling ocean. No land was in sight.

Jack quickly dropped to his chair again and picked up the remains of his lunch as he heard footsteps in the passageway. Then he saw a gigantic blob of darkness silhouetted against the bars of his cell.

"Just wanted to make sure you was all right," came The Claw's growl.

"I'm not cooked yet," Jack said with attempted cheerfulness. "Say, Claw, what's the idea of stopping here?"

"Worried?" The Claw asked. "No, Powder, we ain't reached that coral reef yet. We're just waitin' for that PB to show up. If you listen maybe you'll be able to hear the motors when it comes 'longside."

The Claw rattled the door to make sure it was tightly fastened and then he turned to go.

"Well, as long as you're still salted down okay, I'll move along," he said.

"I'm doing quite well—thank you—under the circumstances," Jack replied. "But I do much better when you're not around."

The Claw laughed unpleasantly.

"My my! Wotta cheerful disposition," he said as he walked away.

As soon as Jack heard The Claw go up the ladder to the deck, he moved his chair to the window. A moment before, when he stood beside the port, one of the bars had seemed loose. He examined the bar with care. Only a single, rusty bolt held it in place. He needed something to cut that bolt.

A smile spread over Jack's face as he remembered he had something! In his pocket was the hardest substance in the world—a diamond. It could cut steel like a file! It would even cut glass!

Jack dug into his pocket. A look of dismay crossed his face as he found the pocket empty. Then he felt the ring in his other pocket and the old smile reappeared.

Holding the diamond to the light, Jack marveled at its size and beauty. But there was no time to waste. He set to work cutting the bolt that held the bar across the porthole.

For almost an hour he worked, making slow headway. It was hard to hold the ring firmly. Then he heard the hum of motors in the distance. The four-motored patrol bomber was arriving just in time to fit into Jack's plan.

If Jack could get out of the porthole soon after the plane landed, he might find it temporarily unguarded. That patrol bomber would be just the thing for him to use in his escape!

The metal bolt and the tiny ring burned and numbed his fingers, but Jack kept on working. At last the bolt was worn almost in two. With a supreme effort, Jack twisted it off. Then he caught hold of the rusty bar and, throwing all of his weight on it, bent it back to the bulk-head. Luckily it was a small, narrow bar.

Now only a pane of thick glass separated Jack from the open air. Jack might use the chair to smash the glass, but the sound possibly would be heard on deck.

The diamond must be used to cut away the glass.

The roar of the four-motored bomber was deafening now, and suddenly Jack caught his first glimpse of it through the dirty porthole. A moment later it landed gracefully on the sea and taxied toward the yacht.

"What a plane!" Jack said admiringly as he gazed at the craft through the porthole.

But there would be time to feast his eyes on the plane later. Jack redoubled his efforts to cut the glass. The ring had dug a deep scratch around the glass now and Jack was ready to remove the pane.

Picking up his discarded coat, Jack spread it against the glass. Then he pressed against the center of the glass with the palm of his hand. There was a sharp crack as the glass broke. It fell outward and dropped with a faint splash into the water of the ocean.

For several precious seconds Smilin' Jack stood in front of the opening, gulping refreshing lungfuls of cool air. But he could spend little time enjoying this luxury. Quickly he turned his full attention to escape. The Claw might return on another inspection trip at any moment and the open porthole would be quickly discovered.

With his coat wrapped around his hand, Jack pried loose the remaining bits of glass from the frame of the porthole. When he had finished, he stripped off the remainder of his clothing.

To measure his chances, he thrust his head through the opening.

It was the smallest porthole he had ever seen, but there was a chance he could make it. At least it was worth a try.

He wormed one shoulder through with only a little difficulty, but the second shoulder was a problem. At last, squirming and twisting, and at the cost of some skin, he made it.

Bracing his muscular arms against the side of the ship he drew his chest through the opening.

"Lucky for me I don't have a big waistline," he thought grimly.

Inch by inch he eased his body, glistening with perspiration, through the small opening. Then he stopped, his hips stuck fast.

A momentary panic swept over Smilin' Jack as it seemed that he could not move either forward or backward.

"Good night!" he muttered. "I'm in for it now. I'm caught."

He rested a second and then strained with all his might. His body moved a fraction of an inch as the frame of the porthole gouged deep into the flesh of his hips. Every move he made scraped off some skin. But he had to go on. He worked and struggled painfully.

Perspiration flowed from every pore in his body and it was this moisture that did the trick. Slowly at first and then faster his body slid through the opening. The sharp edges of the porthole cut less deeply and Jack was freeing himself. Suddenly his body slipped forward and he plunged headfirst into the water beside the ship.

The cooling dive put new energy into his muscles, even though the salt bit at the bleeding scratches made by the sides of the porthole. He was free!

Jack rose, gulped in a lungful of air and then sank under the waves again. Swimming under water and rising only to gasp air, he moved toward the patrol bomber which was being refueled at the stern of the yacht.

One man, undoubtedly one of the two spies who had stolen the naval aircraft, was on the wing holding the hose in the fuel tank.

"Lucky there's only one to deal with," Jack thought as he came up on the far side of the plane.

His arm shot up and caught the wing strut. For a moment he rested and then drew his body out of the water. A slow stealthy climb brought Jack to the wing.

The man on the wing heard the noise as Jack pulled himself to his feet, but before he had a chance to realize what was happening or give a cry of alarm, Jack had lunged forward with his fists swinging. A left-right, one-two blow to the jaw sent the spy staggering off the wing and into the water.

The shout of alarm released by the falling man was echoed aboard the yacht.

"Powder's escaped!" shrieked a voice from the bridge. "Get guns!"

Diving into the cockpit, Jack slammed on the starters and throttle. The engine caught instantly. Four propellers churned the air. The craft swung around, but it did not seem to move.

It was anchored!

Suddenly there was a crash of glass as a rifle bullet smashed through the cabin of the bomber. Jack would be riddled in a second or two by the shooting from the deck of the yacht.

Grimly Jack grasped the controls of the aircraft and swung it around so that the back-wash from the propellers of the four motors swept the deck.

The firing suddenly ceased as a miniature hurricane swept across the yacht. Good shooting was impossible in the teeth of that gale.

The maneuver gave Jack a chance to locate and release the anchor control. The patrol bomber shot forward like an arrow across the water. In a few more seconds it began to lift and skimmed upward into the air.

Jack glanced back, feeling safe for the first time since he had been made a prisoner by The Head. But Jack's troubles were not ended.

The crane on the yacht was lowering one of the two seaplanes to the water in preparation for pursuit.

Jack's position now was serious. He was familiar with the seaplanes and he knew that they had six synchronized machine guns in the wings. Without a gunner to fight off the smaller and swifter machine, Jack would be at the mercy of his pursuer.

The Seaplane Tailed the Larger Plane

With this realization, Jack checked his climb. There was no time to gain altitude now—he had to put as much distance as possible between himself and the seaplane.

The seaplane came skimming over the water. In a moment it took the air and tailed the larger and slower craft. It seemed to gain with the speed of a bullet, in spite of the fact that Jack had his throttle wide open.

All chances of escape were fading. In a few more minutes the white web of tracer bullets would begin weaving a death trap for Smilin' Jack.

But danger breeds ideas. The instinct of self-preservation is strongest when it is needed most.

Smilin' Jack's brain did a ground loop and landed with a three-point idea.

Jack's hand went forward throwing the robot pilot into operation. The American's face was set grimly as he released the controls of the craft. It was sailing straight ahead, a perfect target for bullets from the little hornet on its tail, but Jack was willing to take a chance that the pursuer would hold his fire in hopes Jack would surrender. The patrol bomber was much too valuable a military prize to destroy if it could be captured in one piece.

"If this trick doesn't throw 'em off my tail, the surprise will!" Jack muttered to himself.

He left the cockpit and moved along the catwalk to the tail turret. Crouching behind the machine gun in the turret he trained it on the seaplane.

The pursuer was creeping closer. It was near enough now to turn loose with its six "stingers" and riddle the larger craft to shreds.

Jack's finger squeezed the trigger of the turret gun. A deafening roar rattled in his ears. The smell of powder swept into his nostrils. A chain of empty shell-cases dropped from the tail of the bomber.

The spray of bullets struck the seaplane with crippling force. The little machine seemed to shudder with the impact. It wobbled from its course. Desperately it tried to come out of its uncontrollable slip. Then a black streamer of smoke began to rise from the engine and red tongues of flame licked at the fuselage.

The pursuing craft suddenly went completely out of control and fell like a wounded duck straight toward the waters of the Pacific Ocean.

Striking the sea with a tremendous crash, it turned over on its nose and settled on the waves with roaring flames climbing up the frame of the cockpit.

A feeling of pity swept over Jack for the man inside that plane, even though the pursuer might have been ready to send Jack to a similar fate. More than likely the pilot was Jim, the man who had flown Jack to meet the Claw. It was the end of a long career of dishonest flying—dope running, smuggling, and, finally, betrayal of his country.

"He deserved it," Jack said grimly.

CHAPTER SEVEN

Having made good his escape, Smilin' Jack had only a vague idea where he was, but he knew there were many islands in this part of the Pacific. If he could find one of them inhabited, he would land and get in touch with American authorities on the mainland.

There were two reasons for not using the radio on the patrol bomber until he was in a friendly port: The Head still had another seaplane, faster and more maneuverable than the big ship, and there might be other enemy planes within striking distance.

Jack's job was to get the bomber back to America or, failing that, to destroy it so that it would not fall in enemy hands. He hoped that he would be within range of rescue when the time came to destroy the plane if that last recourse became necessary.

When an island shoved its head above the horizon Jack nosed the bomber toward it. Leeward of a jungle-fringed shore on the southeastern end of the isle was a lagoon. From the air the place looked uninhabited, but there might be some people living there. At any rate, Jack could replenish his fresh water supply and rest a while before flying northward and eastward toward the United States.

Jack donned clothing he found aboard the plane: a

pair of dark blue trousers, a light shirt and some shoes stored in a locker. There also was food—iron rations—but the water was low.

The bomber circled the lagoon. It was small and apparently rarely used, but it looked sufficient to harbor the bomber, unless hidden reefs were under the water. Still, a seaplane with a very small draft might glide safely over water so shallow as to be dangerous for a ship.

Down, down, Jack nosed the plane. He sideslipped to check his speed and then straightened out. The bottom of the ship touched the waves and then rested on the water, skimming toward the sandy beach that ran to the water's edge from the jungle.

"I'm goin' to make it!" Jack beamed as these words sang triumphantly in his brain.

But hardly had the words left his mouth when there was a grinding crash. The forward motion ceased abruptly and the plane swung around. From below, salt water surged into the cockpit.

The patrol bomber was sinking!

In spite of the plane's shallow draft, Jack must have hit a submerged reef as he tried to beach his ship on this lonely island. The rocks apparently had torn away most of the bottom, and the inrushing sea water could not be stemmed.

Dropping the controls Jack clambered out of the cockpit just ahead of the rising water. He took stock of the situation quickly. The shore was not far away and he could make it. The doomed bomber was useless to Jack and equally lost to the enemy.

Without further delay Smilin' Jack plunged into the ocean and struck out for shore.

As he struck the water he remembered sharks, but it was too late to change his mind. The thought seemed to put strength into his muscles as he breasted the waves. Each ripple of the ocean around him seemed to be a fin charging toward him; each tug of the ocean on his body seemed to be the current caused by the closing of saw-toothed jaws.

Then Jack's feet struck bottom. He pulled himself, wet and bedraggled, up on the white sands. Looking back he saw only a ripple where the giant bomber had been a few minutes before. His only means of transportation was on the bottom: Jack was shipwrecked three thousand miles from home.

"Now I know how Robinson Crusoe felt," Jack muttered to himself.

But Crusoe was lucky. He had rescued tools and supplies from his ship before it sank. Jack didn't have even a hammer.

All he could see of the island was utterly desolate. His eyes swept the beach.

Wait a minute—what was that?

Something seemed to move near the fringe of palm trees. It dived into a clump of brush at the edge of the beach. Jack tensed. The figure had looked human. If it was friendly, why did it hide? If it was a foe, why didn't it attack? An attack, at least, would be relief from a disturbing uncertainty.

The swaying brush ceased moving. A deadly silence settled over the beach.

Was the figure a native? Jack recalled reading somewhere that while cannibalism was generally believed to be stamped out, it might still persist among some primitive savages in out-of-the-way places. The American aviator had visions of himself going into a pot to provide a feast for a king with a bone ornament in his nose.

Well, cannibals or not, Jack had to find out—he could stand the suspense no longer. Cupping his hands he shouted toward the thick curtain of vegetation:

"Hi, you! Come out of that brush!"

Again the branches of the shrubs stirred as something moved. Something was there—an intelligent something that could understand the English language.

A piece of driftwood lay on the beach. Jack stooped, picking it up as he advanced to find out what was hiding in the shrubs. He went forward determinedly, half crouching, ready to meet any sort of attack.

The stirring of the green leaves grew violent.

"No, no!" came a startled cry from the undergrowth. "Fat Stuff he come out. He surrender!"

The brush parted and from the undergrowth stepped a puff-cheeked, pot-bellied man.

A native? Yes. His brown skin and black hair were unmistakably those of an islander. A cannibal? No. There was a pleasantly good-natured gleam in the man's countenance, even though the fellow's eyes rolled with fear and his mouth was agape with fright.

But these first impressions were swept away by another feature that struck Jack with the force of a blow.

This man wore the striped clothing and monkey hat of a convict!

"Who—what—?"

The native did not seem to hear Jack's words. An expression of relief enveloped the man's whole body as he noticed Jack's wet clothing and bedraggled appearance. Possibly this fat, puff-cheeked native had expected something quite different. At any rate, the hunted look vanished and the gape of his mouth narrowed into a grin.

"Oh!" the native exclaimed. "You stranger here."

"You're a convict!" Jack said accusingly. "Where did you escape from?"

The hunted look returned.

"Don't sendum Fat Stuff back to Death Rock prison!" he pleaded.

"Death Rock prison?" Jack had never heard of the place.

"Fat Stuff no likum work in sulphur mine. Fat Stuff likum fish. Him no likum work at all."

This man who called himself Fat Stuff looked harmless, yet many criminals had innocent baby-faces and disarming ways. Fat Stuff might be a convicted murderer. Fat Stuff had lost his jacket, but the striped trousers were enough to prove that he had been in a prison. Aiding a prisoner to escape would make Jack a criminal too, but he did need help—badly.

"We'll talk that over later," Jack decided. "Right now you can be of help to me. Where's the closest settlement on this island?"

Fat Stuff shook his head.

"No go there," he said. "Limehouse throwum you in prison too. Him need convicts. Him short."

"That's ridiculous, Fat Stuff—if that's your name," Jack said. "I haven't done anything to be thrown in prison for—unless—say, what country owns this island?"

Fat Stuff shrugged his shoulders.

"Death Rock owned by man. Him toss everybody in jail who come here."

Fat Stuff spoke earnestly and convincingly, but the meaning his words conveyed was too outlandish. In any civilized community (except one ruled by Nazis or Japs) men aren't imprisoned for no reason at all. The oversized native probably was fabricating the tale.

"I've got to get something to eat and find a radio station," Jack went on. "I'm in no position now to capture a fugitive from justice. I'll make a bargain with you. Direct me to the settlement and I'll go there alone. I'm not promising that I won't tell the authorities where I saw you, but I'm unarmed and I could hardly be expected to bring in a desperate convict without the proper—er—equipment."

Fat Stuff listened and smiled.

"Good bargain," he agreed cheerfully.

"*No* bargain!" came a new voice.

From the palm trees behind Fat Stuff a white man

appeared. His long, angular body was impeccably dressed in a linen suit and on his head was a tropical sun helmet. A hypocritical smile flicked underneath his long and pointed nose in his dish-face. He held an automatic rather carelessly in his hand, pointed in the general direction of Jack and Fat Stuff.

Still smiling cynically the newcomer stepped out on the beach and approached Jack and the native. Fat Stuff trembled violently.

But the newcomer's eyes were not fixed on the escaped convict—they were fixed on Jack.

"My word!" he exclaimed. *"Powder!"*

Smilin' Jack's heart sank. The name Powder carried with it certain unpleasant implications. If anyone ever deserved to be behind prison bars it was Powder Pellet.

The dish-faced white man stopped half a dozen paces from Jack. He still held the automatic carelessly, but Jack caught a cruel look in the man's eyes hinting that he would not begrudge using it—with care.

"So you finally decided to come back to see Limehouse, did you?" the white man asked. "I suppose The Head sent you. How'd you get here, anyhow? Your clothing's all wet—maybe you swum!"

Limehouse laughed mirthlessly.

"I came by plane, Limehouse," Jack said, in Powder's voice. "But it struck a rock in the lagoon and sank."

Limehouse's evil grin broadened.

"Now isn't that too bad! If this gun should go off accidentally, our friend The Head would never know you

Limehouse Held the Automatic Carelessly

landed here at all."

Limehouse's two references to The Head gave Smilin' Jack an inkling that this man, whoever he was, had at one time associated with the international spy. Limehouse therefore would not be above shooting just for the fun of it.

"But I don't think I shall kill you yet, Powder," he went on, allowing the muzzle of the automatic to drop slightly. He turned to the native. "Well, Fat Stuff, your freedom didn't last long."

"What did I do for-um go to prison?" Fat Stuff asked plaintively.

"Do? *Do!*" Limehouse roared with laughter. "You got caught, that's what. Jim caught you, just like Powder caught so many on the mainland. Only difference between Jim an' Powder is, Jim knocked over natives. He got easy ones. Powder used Mickey Finns to nab sailors on the mainland."

"You take-um me back?" Fat Stuff asked, with a panicky look in his eyes. "I die sure!"

"Lie down on the beach, Fat Stuff," Limehouse ordered curtly. "Keep quiet. One false move an' I'll plug you, even if it'll make me another man short."

Limehouse's references to Mickey Finns and being "short" bewildered Jack. Something very strange was going on—something unholy.

Fat Stuff was prone on the beach now, and Limehouse turned to Jack.

"You know, Powder," Limehouse began, "there's a

mite of unfinished business 'tween you an' me."

Jack's heart sank. Whatever had taken place between Limehouse and Powder was a closed book to Jack, who had not even known of this man's existence a few minutes ago. Bluffing might serve, but Limehouse might catch on at any time that this was not Powder Pellet standing before him.

"Unfinished business?" Jack asked, stalling.

"Don't act so innocent, Powder," Limehouse said sneeringly. "I'm referring to that diamond ring you stole from the countess. Big as a forty-five bullet. Where is it?"

"Oh!"

Jack knew where that diamond was. Limehouse had given him a hint, after all. The diamond was in the clothing he had left behind on the yacht—in the ring Powder had given Betty to seal their engagement.

"Where is it?"

There was a threatening undertone in Limehouse's voice, but Jack was unshaken.

"I got bumped on the head when the plane hit the reef," Jack said. "It's hard for me to remember."

"Maybe it would make you remember if I put you on Death Rock awhile," Limehouse spoke sharply. "You needn't think you've fooled me, Powder. I know you and The Head have had a falling out. He sent a message to me earlier today telling me the whole story. I sort of figured you'd wind up here because I know you've got a nice little cache of treasure hidden on the island. Money, jewelry and other little trinkets you stole from the men you shanghaied for Death Rock!"

Here was a new revelation concerning the man that Betty Brown had expected to marry. He was engaged in shanghaiing men for Death Rock—whatever that might be.

"The Head's comin' here soon, Powder," Limehouse went on. "What he has in store for you ain't none of my business, but it's plenty of yours."

Cold perspiration broke from Jack's pores. The Head might have any number of horrors in store for the man he believed to be Powder.

"Now I'm a reasonable man, Powder," Limehouse went on. "I don't like to see my friends suffer. Just show me where your treasure is, an' I'll forget I ever saw you."

So Limehouse wanted to be bribed! The scoundrel must think Jack was easily duped to offer such a proposition. From Limehouse's manner, it was not hard to guess that murder was a trifling thing to him. As soon as Jack uncovered a treasure, Limehouse would shoot and forget that he ever saw anyone called "Powder."

On the other hand, if Jack didn't appear to agree to the plan, The Head would make matters much more complicated.

"Okay," Jack said. "You can have the treasure."

Limehouse turned to the heavy man lying on the sand.

Slowly the huge native rose to his feet.

"Turn around!"

Fat Stuff groaned, as Jack watched the proceedings

without realizing at first what they meant.

"Sorry to do this, Fat Stuff—but where a fortune is involved one can't let everybody in on it."

Jack suddenly realized that Limehouse was about to kill this friendless native.

"Wait!" Jack cried. "I've a better idea."

Limehouse lowered the gun slightly.

"Well, speak fast—I'm in a hurry to get my hands on that gold."

"That's just it," Jack said. "It's possible we may not find the treasure."

"Maybe you'd rather let The Head play with you?" Limehouse suggested.

"No, but I'm not sure I know the exact spot," Jack said. "And someone may have found it already. Why not keep an ace in the hole? Leave Fat Stuff tied here and then you can collect the reward on him if I don't turn up the treasure."

Limehouse, to Jack's surprise, seemed to consider the proposition. Jack had been stalling, hoping for a chance to make a break or to overpower this beady-eyed man. But the suggestion, advanced by Jack in the face of uncertainties, seemed to be well taken.

"M-m-m!" Limehouse said. "Something in what you say. I'm short of prisoners an' even a worthless slob like Fat Stuff can't be spared very well. Yes, Powder, thank you for lookin' out for my interests. Fat Stuff *will* be an ace in the hole. But remember, in case you're looking out for any tricks, The Head will pay a fancy price for you, too."

Limehouse took some handcuffs from his pocket and put them on Fat Stuff's wrists. Then, with Limehouse forcing his two prisoners to walk ahead, they entered the jungle. A short distance away they came upon an old model touring car. Into this he forced Fat Stuff; then the native's legs were tightly bound with rope, which Limehouse found in the car.

From a trunk on the side of the car Limehouse pulled out a pick and shovel which he tossed over his shoulder.

"Lead the way, Powder!" he ordered, pointing the pistol at Jack.

Without the slightest idea where he was going, Smilin' Jack plunged into the jungle. The task was difficult. He was supposed to know this area but he had never visited it before.

For several minutes they walked through thick undergrowth.

"Just a minute, Powder," Limehouse called. "You needn't try to stall. I know the treasure is somewhere around here. I followed you a couple of times, but you always eluded me here. You know where the gold is. Show me."

Jack had to do some fast thinking and unrehearsed acting.

"Oh—why—sure—it's been so long since I was here, I didn't recognize the place!" Jack stammered, looking around. "There it is!"

Jack pointed toward a giant palm tree about a hundred feet ahead.

"There's the place. We start there and walk a straight line toward that tall peak—"

A glimpse of a basalt spire through the trees gave Jack his lead, and he strode from the foot of the palm on a line toward it.

"—ninety paces—then a right turn—"

Jack could hardly keep this up very long. If he could only stall Limehouse until after dark, he'd have a much better chance to escape. It was already late afternoon—night could not be far from falling.

"Yes, yes!" Limehouse said impatiently. "What next?"

"Now fifty paces to—to that sharp rock!" Jack spotted the rock just in time.

"Yes, yes—is that where the treasure is?" Limehouse asked eagerly.

"—Ah—no," Jack said. "We have to wait till after dark and line this rock with the North Star—and then—"

A cunning gleam came into Limehouse's eyes.

"Dark, hey? Powder, if you're plannin' a double-cross you're just as good as in The Head's torture chamber right now!"

Limehouse was pointing the gun directly at Smilin' Jack's heart.

Jack knew he couldn't stall much longer.

"Well, maybe I can find it without the North Star," Jack said. "Yes—that way is north."

Jack counted off twenty-five paces from the rock and asked for the shovel. There was nothing else to do but to start digging in the spot he had selected entirely at random.

The eager and impatient Limehouse stood to one side with the gun pointed at Jack as the hole grew deeper and deeper—and the shadows grew longer and longer.

"Better hurry," Limehouse said.

Jack had to do something. A desperate plan began forming in his mind. The next time the shovel blade struck a rock—

The blade rang against a buried chunk of lava.

"Look!" Jack exclaimed. "I've found it!".

Limehouse sprang forward for a look. As he came close to Jack the shovel came up, hurling loose sand full in the face of the man holding the gun.

Ducking a bullet which crashed into a tree behind him, Jack sprang from the hole and dashed for freedom.

Momentarily blinded by the sand, Limehouse roared with anger. He tried to brush his eyes clear, and then, howling with rage, fired aimlessly at the hazy figure of Smilin' Jack he saw darting into the jungle.

Only a few more steps and Jack would be completely out of sight, but the bullets were whizzing close to him, panging off rocks and burying themselves in the palm trees.

The automatic crashed again. This bullet accidentally struck its mark. With a scream of pain, Smilin' Jack stumbled and fell in the grass of the jungle.

A moment later he rose. His leg felt as if it had been kicked by a mule, but he knew it was only a flesh wound.

Desperately, Jack tried to drag himself into the dense undergrowth of the jungle. Each move cost him pain, but he had to get away before Limehouse spotted him.

Limehouse, however, had heard Jack's cry, and, before Jack could hide, he had run toward the spot where Jack had fallen.

"Oh!" he cried spotting Jack crawling into the brush. "There you are! You can't double-cross *me* an' get away with it!"

Limehouse's arm shot down, seized Jack's shoulder and jerked him back from the brush. Jack looked upward into the muzzle of the automatic.

"Say your prayers, Powder!" Limehouse snarled. "An automatic is about to be emptied in your face!"

CHAPTER EIGHT

DEATH ROCK

For a moment Smilin' Jack stared unflinchingly into the barrel of the pistol. It held steadily for a second and then seemed to turn away from Jack's gaze.

"Well?" Jack asked, stubbornly. "What're you waiting for? Get it over with. It'll be better than meeting The Head again."

Limehouse's mouth twisted sideways in an abortive smile.

"No," he said studiously, "shootin' is too easy for you, Powder. I'd enjoy turnin' you over to The Head, to die by inches. Then you'll realize how foolish you were not to lead me to the treasure, you double-crosser."

Limehouse rose and jerked Jack to his feet. The wound pained Jack considerably, but he did not utter a sound.

"But before The Head gets you, I think I'll give you a taste of my own revenge," he said. "I'll put you in Death Rock to rot for awhile with some of the men you shanghaied from the mainland. No doubt that will help you decide to take me to the buried gold."

The name of Death Rock sounded bad enough. Jack had heard enough to realize it was some sort of a prison. Fat Stuff must have escaped from there. But why were men shanghaied for this prison? Even the hardest-hearted warden in the world does not solicit prisoners, nor have them kidnaped so that his prison will be full. There was something deeply and wickedly mysterious about Death Rock.

But what made it appear less savory than ever to Smilin' Jack was the fact that Powder, the man Jack was impersonating, had assisted in kidnaping prisoners for this undeserved punishment. The wrath of these unjustly incarcerated men might lead to a terrible revenge if they recognized Powder as the villain responsible for their plight.

Limehouse released his hold, and Jack, weak from pain, dropped to the ground.

Limehouse pulled back Jack's torn trouser leg and glanced at the wound.

"Bad luck, Powder," he said. "The wound ain't serious. It would be lucky for you if it was."

Then Limehouse pulled a handkerchief from his pocket and handed it to Smilin' Jack.

"Bandage your wound," he ordered. "It'd make me sad if you cashed in your chips before we got to Death Rock prison."

Night was falling rapidly now, bringing the darkness Jack had needed for his escape, but escape no longer was possible since Jack had a painfully wounded leg. As inhumane as Death Rock prison was painted by Limehouse, medical treatment at least would be given there, Jack reasoned.

Jack's leg was growing stiff as he managed to get to his

feet at last. Limehouse refused to aid his prisoner, pre-
ferring to watch Jack's agony as they retraced their steps
through the jungle to the car. When, at last, they reached
the machine, they found Fat Stuff fast asleep. The native did not let his troubles keep him awake.

"You two will bring a nice reward," Limehouse gloated as Jack climbed laboriously into the car. "An escaped
prisoner brings as large a premium as a new one. You,
Powder, will bring a double reward. You are both a new
prisoner and a man on whom The Head has placed a
price."

Jack turned the words over in his mind. The statement
that rewards were paid for new prisoners sounded
strangely like slavery. But slavery had no proper place
in the modern world. This must be a place outside the
pale.

Limehouse tied the arms of the two prisoners and took
the wheel of the car. The machine followed the jungle
road until it reached a barren chain of hills along the
eastern shore. Here the road began a winding ascent. The
hills grew steeper until they rose precipitously out of the
sea, seeming to form a rampart against the lashing waves
of the ocean.

The highway itself seemed to be only a ledge carved
in the side of the vertical cliff.

For several miles the car chugged up the steep road,
then at last it came in view of several buildings surrounded by a high wall on which searchlights gleamed.

"There it is!" Limehouse exclaimed. "Home, sweet

"There Is Death Rock Prison!" Limehouse Said

home—Death Rock prison! The inferno of the South Sea Islands—the hotel where guests enter vertically an' come out horizontally."

Even at a distance the prison had a bleak and cruel look. The moonlight and the glow of the searchlights created a ghastly illusion of something unreal, as in a nightmare. The buildings were perched on the side of the mountain, with the sea directly below and high cliff walls above. The only approach was along the narrow high- way on which the car was traveling.

The car stopped in front of the gate. Limehouse untied his prisoners and, brandishing his gun, ordered them out.

A challenge came from a tower at the gate and Lime- house shouted an answer:

"It's all right, guard!" he called. "Open up. This is Limehouse returnin' with a couple o' prodigal sons."

A gruff voice shouted indistinguishable words behind the wall and a moment later the huge gate swung open. Jack caught a glimpse of a barren courtyard, patrolled by armed guards beyond.

"Okay, you birds," Limehouse said. "Get goin'."

Fat Stuff pulled Smilin' Jack's arm over his shoulder. "Lean on Fat Stuff," he told Jack. "Him help you walk."

"Thanks, Fat Stuff," Jack said.

As they approached the gate, Limehouse turned to his prisoners and remarked tauntingly:

"Well, boys, you'd better take a deep breath—this is your last chance to breathe free air."

Jack heard Fat Stuff growl deep in his chest. But the sound was not loud enough for Limehouse to hear.

The huge gate clanked behind them as they passed into the prison courtyard. Jack underwent a feeling of helplessness as he realized that escape now was cut off. His life was sealed among the living dead of a South Sea island prison: a concentration camp of the vilest kind.

Limehouse directed them toward a large central building, and the two men were taken through a corridor to a large office where a light was burning.

"We'll see the commandant now," Limehouse said. "Then I'll be sure of gettin' full credit for you two."

Guards seized Jack roughly and, paying no attention to his wound, fingerprinted him and then thrust him stumbling into a room where a bald, foreign-looking man in uniform sat at a desk.

Limehouse, with a self-satisfied grin on his ugly face, was standing near by.

"This is the new one, sir," Limehouse explained. "Maybe you recognize our ol' friend an' former helper— Powder Pellet."

"Ah! So it is!"

"You are making a serious mistake," Jack said. "As a matter of fact, I am not Powder Pellet. If you will communicate with the nearest United States consulate I can quickly establish my identity. My name is not Pellet. I am Smilin' Jack Martin, an American aviator."

"Ha, ha!" Limehouse laughed. "You are surely smart-

er than that, Powder. You admitted to me that you were
Powder."

"My employer has placed a price on your head," the
commandant said.

"Your employer? Isn't this a government prison?"

"Ah, yes," the commandant said. "A certain South
American official furnishes us with convicts to work our
mines. We lease the labor, as it were, Mr. Pellet. But the
government official is too humane. He does not wish to
see the scum of the earth he sends us, die. Therefore we
have to replace the men who die with live ones. There
always is an opening here for new talent, as you well
know."

"He ought to know," Limehouse laughed. "Powder
has brought plenty of shanghaied men here in his airplane."

Now Jack was beginning to understand. The Head
owned this island and leased convicts for labor, through
the connivance of some corrupt politician. Unhealthy
conditions at the prison made the lives of the prisoners
short and in order to avoid the cutting off of his labor
supply, The Head had taken upon himself the replace-
ment of men who had died. Fat Stuff had been kidnaped probably from a near-by island. Powder, whom Jack
was impersonating, had shanghaied men from South
American ports. More than ever, Jack sensed the mon-
strous nature of the man known as The Head.

"But I am not Powder!" Jack insisted.

"You lie!" shouted the commandant. "Your features

and the brand on your left hand are proof enough for anyone that you are Powder Pellet."

Fat Stuff now entered and offered his support for Jack. The commandant seemed to notice for the first time that Jack was wounded.

"He resisted arrest an' I had to plug him," Limehouse explained.

Fat Stuff looked expectantly at Jack.

"Take him to the hospital and then throw him in the bull pen with the rest of the convicts," the commandant said with a smile. "Powder ought to find some of his *old friends* there. Men he brought here!"

Fat Stuff helped carry Jack to the hospital.

"Your name not Powder, but Jack?" he asked.

Smilin' Jack nodded.

"Very strange," he said. "Powder not popular here. It will be hard to make others believe."

"I hope we can," Jack said, resolving that, somehow, he must survive whatever was in store for him at Death Rock.

"Jack, why you no tell commandant how Limehouse try to make you tell of buried treasure?" Fat Stuff asked.

"What's the use, Fat Stuff?" Jack asked. "My word would be worthless against Limehouse's. Besides, the commandant might have a few greedy ideas himself and try to make me tell *him* where the treasure was hidden."

The prison doctor quickly confirmed that Jack's wound was of a minor nature. The injury was cleaned and treated, and Jack was placed in the infirmary.

In this hospital ward Jack began to learn more about the nature of Death Rock prison. As he had suspected, the prisoners were farmed out to a syndicate owned by The Head. The prisoners were employed in sulphur mines, where convicts died by scores in the scorching heat and unhealthy atmosphere.

The government was doubtless unaware or unwilling, because of political corruption, to take cognizance of these conditions. Jack suspected bribery. At any rate The Head was required to return only the number of prisoners each year corresponding with the number whose terms had expired. Inefficiency, or crookedness, seemed to cause the proper officials to overlook the fact that the prisoners who returned seldom had features or fingerprints corresponding with the men whose names they bore. Even in the United States such corruption was not unknown, as was revealed when the guilty officials were brought to justice.

The Head, of course, was allowed a small "loss" in prisoners due to death. But he was forced to resort to kidnaping tactics in order to prevent an investigation as to the treatment of the convicts in his charge. The convicts themselves knew of the conditions and considered their chances of freedom virtually zero.

After about three days of treatment, Jack's leg had almost healed and Commandant Trefwitz ordered the prisoner transferred to the "bull pen."

As he was being escorted to the pen, Jack caught sullen looks from other prisoners. Snarling taunts were hurled at him from evil, distorted faces behind the bars of cells.

"What a reputation Powder is giving me!" Jack thought to himself. "Nearly every man in this prison is his enemy!"

But the feeling could hardly be condemned. The real "Powder" had evidently brought by violent means many of these men to this island of living death.

"Lookie what's here, boys!" came a cry as Jack was thrust into an enclosure filled with other convicts.

A degenerate-looking being thrust his features close to Jack's.

"Remember me, Powder?" he said. "Remember that doped whisky you fed me in Chiclavo?"

A snarl sounded behind Jack and a wizened little man came charging toward the American with doubled fists.

"Let me at him!" he cried.

The first convict suddenly thrust his body between Jack and the smaller man.

"Wait, Lizard!"

Lizard tried to fight off the larger man.

"Let me at him, Slab!" he cried. "I'm gonna get even wit' him for de time he slugged me in Guayaquil an' brought me here!"

"Take it easy, Lizard," Slab cautioned. "If we start a rumpus an' th' guards hear us, they'll turn scaldin' water on us sure!"

Another sprang forward and helped Slab check Lizard's murderous intentions.

"We'll have a much better chance to settle with Powder when we're back in the mines," Slab said hoarsely, casting an evil glance at Jack.

"Yeah," said his helper. "De guards ain't so watchful t'ere. Ya can do anyt'ing ya like to Powder den. But remember one t'ing—" the convict glanced around the room "—no fair killin' him till we've all had our toin at gettin' even wit' him!"

Jack's heart sank. If the sulphur mines didn't get him, his fellow prisoners would.

Later in the day Limehouse appeared with an armed guard and called Jack from the bull pen.

"The commandant desires your presence in the courtroom, Powder," Limehouse announced. "He told me to inform you that you are convict No. M-6000. It's a lucky number—the last man who had it wasn't here very long."

Sensing from the ugly inflection that M-6000 had not been released, Jack retorted:

"He must have had a drag to get such a distinctive number."

The unscrupulous prison official chuckled mirthlessly.

"I'll take some of that insolence out of you, No. M-6000," he said. "I'll make a lot of changes in you. Those pretty curls will go first—you won't look so handsome with your head shaved."

Jack smiled to himself. When his blonde hair was shaved away, his scalp would sprout locks of quite a different color—chestnut brown. "Powder" would become a different person than Limehouse expected.

Commandant Trefwitz sat silently on the bench as Jack was taken into the court room. He cleared his throat and addressed the prisoner in a stern tone:

"I've examined the records in your case, M-6000. I find that you have no credit marks and your recent attempt to escape demands the addition of another ten years to your sentence. The time must be spent at hard labor in the sulphur mines."

A malevolent laugh came from Limehouse as he took Jack by the arm.

"Same as a death sentence!" he said. "Ten years in the furnace of a South Sea sulphur mine."

"I might fool you," Jack said grimly. "I might be able to stand the heat."

"Oh, but the heat ain't all that gets you, my dear friend," Limehouse spoke, mockingly. "There's also the sulphur dust—but you'll find out. Now we'll see about some new clothing, more in keepin' with your position."

Jack was taken to the prison tailor shop.

Without ceremony, trousers, shoes, and coat were handed to Smilin' Jack and he was ordered gruffly to try them on. Limehouse, enjoying himself to the utmost, passed taunting remarks with each move Jack made.

"Ain't that a nifty single-breasted, three-button number," the guard said. "Stripes are *so* becomin' to you!"

Jack scowled.

"Now if you don't mind, may I retire to my suite in th' blockhouse and curl up with a nice leg-iron?" he asked.

"Not so fast, my good man," Limehouse said with a curious gleam in his eye. "I've been savin' the best till last. You haven't visited the prison beauty shop yet."

Farther down the corridor was another room in which half a dozen barber chairs were in use. Jack awaited his turn and at last was turned over to a barber of French nationality.

"Oh, Le Mieux," Limehouse spoke to the barber, "our friend, Powder, wants one of your streamlined, air-conditioned head shaves."

Le Mieux smiled.

"Ah! Powder, is it? *Oui, oui,* Monsieur Limehouse! I weel geeve heem ze door-knob special!"

Dressed in his prison stripes, Smilin' Jack seated himself in the barber chair. Le Mieux moved to one side and jerked Jack's right arm up on the arm rest of the chair. There was a quick snap and metal bracelets were fastened on the arm. Le Mieux then fastened the left arm.

"What's the idea of the handcuffs?" Jack demanded.

Limehouse chuckled at the question.

"An old custom here, my friend," the prison guard explained. "They are just in case you should suddenly become fond of Monsieur Le Mieux's razor and try to grab it."

Le Mieux seemed to like his work. His razor lifted aloft and cut a swath down the center of Smilin' Jack's hair.

CHAPTER NINE

CONVICT REVENGE

Possibly because there was such a contrast between Smilin' Jack's rather handsome head and his own vastly different contours, Limehouse seemed to take an unholy delight in watching Le Mieux at work.

"Ah! Right down th' old fairway!" the guard exclaimed, as the barber cut his first groove down the center of Jack's hair. "Your technique is superb, Le Mieux."

"By the way, Limehouse," Jack spoke to the guard, "just why are you cropping me? I noticed some of the other cons—Fat Stuff, for instance—still have their hair."

"A very good question, Powder," Limehouse said, lighting a cigaret. "This service is only for special guests—the ones who are most likely to try to check out without permission. I know Fat Stuff got away once, but he ain't likely to fool us again. But you are dangerous, Powder. The haircut is a tribute to your abilities."

"I still don't see—"

"Ah, but it is quite simple," Limehouse continued. "Did you ever notice how a billiard ball shines when you turn a flashlight on it? Well, supposin' you don't like our hospitality and try to make a break. Just think how a guard's marksmanship would be aided when the prison searchlights beam upon your glistenin' dome!"

Le Mieux quickly finished his job. Jack looked into a mirror to see his head clean and shining—a perfect reflector for a prison searchlight.

Assigned to a cell, Jack spent the night tossing in his bunk. Ten years, plus whatever time was still unserved on M-6000's sentence, remained between him and freedom. From what he had already heard in the bull pen and in the prison infirmary, no man could live that long in the South Sea sulphur mines. Tomorrow he would begin his work in the pits.

Jack had just been able to doze off to sleep when a bell in the cell block rang, announcing the beginning of a new prison day.

With the other prisoners, Jack was herded into the dining room where he was given a breakfast of soggy wheat cakes and coffee. Then he was marched into the bull pen where a hundred or more other convicts were being loaded into trucks for transport to the mine.

Jack noticed that several other convicts, among them Slab and Lizard, who had cast vengeful glances at him the preceding day, were in the group. There also was Fat Stuff, who grinned at his new-found friend.

The sulphur mine was in a deep hollow on the other side of the hill that formed a rampart of the island against the sea. A pit had been opened in the rock and guards were stationed on the rim. These guards carried rifles and their features were those of men who enjoyed seeing fellow beings suffer.

Limehouse seemed to be a supervisor of the guards. He

Jack Set to Work With Fat Stuff

often left the rim to move about in the pit forcing convicts to work harder and to watch for infractions of pris on rules.

Jack was handed a pick and set to work with Fat Stuff, loosening the sulphur in the floor of the pit.

The morning dragged slowly. At noon the men were given only a small meal of thin broth and dried crusts of old bread.

"Dangerous to work on a full stomach," Limehouse explained as he dished the food out to Jack.

During the afternoon Jack began to grow exhausted. He noticed other convicts ready to drop. No wonder men died like flies in this sulphur mine!

Fat Stuff was weak, but he kept swinging his pick.

"Whew!" he said. "Minin' much hard work. No fun, Jack!"

"You said it, Fat Stuff," Jack replied grimly.

The sulphur was embedded in rock just as it had been spewed, centuries before, from a volcano on the island. It was necessary for the sulphur to be separated from the lava before it was loaded into a banking machine which hoisted the mineral from the pit to the ledge above the mine.

"For a man that hasn't done any harder work than jiggle a control stick during the past few years, this is certainly no picnic," Smilin' Jack said as he ceased swinging his pick.

Fat Stuff straightened up and rubbed his lumbar region.

"O-oh!" he groaned. "Fat Stuff back hurtum much!"
You and I are in the same boat," Jack spoke. "And I
used to think I was tired after a double round of golf—
whew!— I've just got to rest a second."

But as Jack leaned on his pick, there came an angry cry
from across the pit.

"Hey, you loafers! Get to work."

Running toward Jack and Fat Stuff was Limehouse,
swinging a blacksnake whip! The whip came down with
a crack and the leash bit deeply into Smilin' Jack's back.

There was to be no rest in this mine. Jack bent his back
and went to work.

"There'll be no loafin' on this job!" the guard announced, with his evil eyes on his newest convict.

Jack caught a glimpse of Lizard and Slab grinning
with amusement at his suffering. They were more or less
toughened to the heavy labor which was tearing and
blistering Jack's hands.

Almost frying in the terrific heat, Jack continued his
work in the dust-filled sulphur quarry. As he began to
think the night would never come, a shrill whistle blew,
signaling that his day's work was finished.

Just nine years and three hundred and sixty-three days
left to go!

"You can stop work now, Powder!" came the tantaliz-
ing voice of Limehouse. "I hope the work isn't too hard
for you—you look a little tired. But you'll feel better after
a hearty meal. This is special diet day."

From experience, Jack knew that Limehouse's little

jokes were full of cruel irony and he was not surprised at the "special diet." It consisted of one slice of bread and a cup of water.

Limehouse took a cruel joy in torturing his prisoners. Although the bullet wound in Jack's leg had not fully healed, he was allowed no shortened hours because of it. His only rest was ten minutes each hour, when the water boy brought some lukewarm water to drink.

Limehouse, too, seemed to look the other way when convicts sought to play their little pranks on Jack. In the role of "Powder," who richly deserved such treatment, Jack could hardly find it in his heart to resent these attempts at vengeance.

Foremost among the pranksters were Slab and Lizard. Once, during the noon lunch period, Jack removed his prison shirt to cool his perspiring chest and shoulders. An instant later the shirt had disappeared. Jack suspected Slab as the thief, but he had no way of proving it—not that it would have helped to be able to prove it.

A few minutes later Fat Stuff noticed Jack laboring shirtless in the hot tropical sun.

"You can't stand that, Jack," Fat Stuff said sympathetically. "Where your shirt?"

"Some louse stole it," Jack replied. "Limehouse won't issue another today. Gosh! This heat is getting me down. I already feel dizzy."

Fat Stuff shook his head.

"Sun burn you up. You die with sun sickness," the native warned. He unbuttoned his own shirt and handed it to Jack. "Here, wear my shirt."

Jack smiled, but waved the proffered garment aside.

"No thanks, Fat Stuff," he said. "I wouldn't take th' shirt off another man's back!"

"No bother!" Fat Stuff insisted, pressing his shirt on Jack. "Here, you take it. Sun no bother me. Me grow up naked in tropics!"

The offer, thus explained, was more than Smilin' Jack could refuse. What Fat Stuff had said was true. The South Sea islander, accustomed to the heat of the tropical sun, could withstand it. Jack on the other hand, had been born in a much different climate, and he was not physically adapted to bear up under the sun's rays without protection.

"You're a big fat Samaritan!" Jack said warmly. "I'm certainly glad I accounted for Jim, the man who brought you here."

"You gottum Jim?" Fat Stuff asked, his eyes widening with happiness.

"I'm pretty sure he was the pilot of the seaplane I shot down when I escaped from The Head," Jack said with a nod.

"You wantum my pants, too?" Fat Stuff asked. "You can havum all my clothes—anythin' you want. Fat Stuff, him your friend for life!"

"I'm your friend too, Fat Stuff," Jack said.

Limehouse was coming toward them with his whip, and Jack quickly donned the shirt and set to work. The pick which Jack wielded was blistering and tearing his hands. The very touch of the wooden handle on Jack's raw palms was maddening torture. To swing the pick was excruciating agony.

Limehouse knew about Jack's hands and he communicated this to the other prisoners, who seemed to enjoy Jack's suffering. Such a fate, they harshly shouted, was too good for the man who had shanghaied so many "prisoners" for Death Rock.

Hour-like minutes piled up their pains until at last it was time for the water boy in the all-too-short rest period the convicts were allowed out of each heavy hour of forced labor.

"Water!" the cry came from parched throats through cracked lips.

Jack put aside his pick and seized the dipper. He gulped down the tepid liquid that seemed to sizzle in his parched throat. Jack sat down and closed his eyes after drinking. He was too tired to notice Lizard and Slab hovering near by. He was too tired to care what mischief they were plotting against him. Even their dirtiest trick would be worth a minute of heavenly rest from that torturing pick.

"Time's up, Powder!" Lizard called out to Jack. "Better get back to work. Limehouse is comin' wit' his whip!"

Jack scrambled to his feet only to perceive that he might have taken a little more time than his ten-minute period for rest.

He reached down for his pick.

Suddenly, from behind Smilin' Jack, a brown hurricane came charging forward. Fat Stuff's body struck Jack and knocked him aside.

"Don't touch pick!" the South Sea islander cried.

Lizard sprang forward, swinging his fists.

"Why, you dirty little meddler!" he cried.

"Fat Stuff see you pour acid on Jack's pick handle!" the native said.

Lizard swung his fist.

"I'll teach you to spoil my revenge!" he said.

The blow landed on Fat Stuff's chin, sending the islander into a heap on the ground.

Jack, picking himself up off the ground, lunged toward Lizard. A single punch, launched from Jack's shoe tops, struck Lizard on the chest. The ugly convict staggered back and then caught himself.

"Dis is what I been waitin' for!" he yelled.

But Jack was ready. He might not be able to swing a pick, but he could fight. His fist swung again. This time the blow caught Lizard on the point of the chin and the convict sank to the ground.

"Stop it, you varmints!" came a coarse voice.

Limehouse, holding his ever-ready automatic, came charging on the scene. He caught Jack by the coat and held him. Another guard, armed with a sub-machine gun, held the other convicts at bay.

"Powder started this riot!" Slab whined as he lifted his friend Lizard to his feet.

Limehouse shook Jack.

"I know! I saw him start it," Limehouse said. "Well,

Powder, accordin' to our penal code, incitin' a prison riot adds two more years to your term, plus the loss of one meal a day for a month."

After one week of work, Jack had "gained" more than one hundred weeks on Death Rock.

Jack's punishment began that night. He was sent supperless to his cell after the prisoners returned from the mine. But Fat Stuff remembered that Jack was penalized for helping him and the native smuggled a crust of bread to Jack.

Jack nibbled at the crust while Fat Stuff explained how he knew Lizard had put acid powder on the pick handle to burn Jack's raw hands.

"Me hear Slab an' Lizard talk," Fat Stuff explained. "Lizard an' Slab hate 'Powder.' Wantum get even."

"Their reaction is understandable," Jack said, "I can't blame them, but I wish I could make them believe I am not 'Powder.' I've tried to explain, but no one will listen."

"They think you lie," Fat Stuff asserted. "But I believe."

"I certainly owe you a lot, Fat Stuff," Jack said warmly. "I don't suppose I'll live long enough to get out of here and repay you, but some day maybe I'll get a chance. You're a real guy."

"You sockum Lizard," the native returned. "You real guy, too."

"By the way, Fat Stuff," Jack asked. "What is your real name?"

Fat Stuff's face blossomed with his infectious grin.

"Real name is Euah-layi-kamil-aroari-yuin-bai-balijaoyra-a-mulung," he said in a sing-song voice.

"Quite a mouthful," Jack said. "Just what does it mean?"

"It mean—Fat Stuff."

Jack, in spite of his misery, grinned—until his cracked lips hurt.

Although Jack resolved to seize the first opportunity to escape that presented itself, there seemed to be no possibility of getting away from the prison. Life on Death Rock was short and uncertain. Clouds of suffocating dust rose day after day in the hot, sun-baked sulphur pit, irritating and burning throats and lungs of the men who labored under the watchful eyes of armed guards.

Jack was growing toughened to the work and he grew more accustomed to the heat, but the sulphur dust seemed to bother him more each day.

Jack's summary dealing with Lizard had helped him in more ways than one. Many of the convicts grew more friendly and seemed to take stock in Jack's tale that he was not Powder. Certainly Jack's powerful blow that felled Lizard had been a far cry from the dandified actions of the man they had known as Powder.

Besides, Jack was one of them, coughing in the sulphur dust, roasting in the sun, unjustly deprived of freedom. Misery made him their fellow.

The slightest breeze made the pit almost unbearable by stirring up the dust that covered the ground. When the wind was strong men coughed from morning until night.

Jack, seized with a coughing spell one day, grew so weak he could hardly hold his pick.

"What trouble, Jack?" Fat Stuff asked.

"That sulphur dust!" Jack coughed. "My lungs feel like they're on fire!"

Even Fat Stuff was coughing.

"Mine, too," the native said. "Sulphur dust much bad for breathe."

A few feet away a convict fell on the ground. Limehouse and an armed guard rushed to his side.

"Poor devil!" Jack said, loudly enough for Limehouse to hear.

The supervisor of the guards sprang to his feet with the ever-ready whip in his hand.

"He's just dead!" Limehouse roared, brandishing his whip. "Another weaklin' who couldn't stand the gaff. Get back to work, so us guards can return to our posts on the bank, where the air is fresh!"

The coughing prisoners went back to their killing labor.

Jack swung his pick silently, thinking. How *could* he get out of here?

Unless he escaped soon, he would die just as that other poor prisoner had died. If Jack died without communicating with headquarters in the United States, all the discoveries about the espionage ring and the Fifth Column bases on the West Coast would never be known by the intelligence corps. Each day of delay might mean losses of ships from submarines fueled at the secret bases.

While Jack pondered one day on some desperate means of escape he heard the first faint drone of a familiar buzz. The sound came from high above the clouds of sulphur dust that filled the air of the pit. But the noise was easily recognizable.

"Maybe I'm going nuts with the heat, Fat Stuff," Jack said in a low voice to his friend. "Maybe I'm having delusions—but I think I hear a plane."

Fat Stuff listened.

"You no nuts," he said, speaking without moving his lips. "It *is* plane."

"Are there planes on this island?"

"Many planes base here on island. Other planes fly over. Me see-um 'Merican warplane with star on wing on patrol sometimes."

An American patrol plane! Jack was closer than he thought to headquarters. If he could only signal the craft—possibly it was a patrol bomber like the plane The Head had tried to steal.

The small spark of hope fanned to a flame in Jack's mind. Once Jack was able to signal the men at the controls of that plane, he could bring about his release—or at least pass on the information he had learned about the spy ring. But Jack would have to work stealthily. If Jack was caught signaling the plane, he would be placed in solitary, where it would be impossible to communicate with the outside world.

Signaling would be a problem with the sulphur dust clouds in the air, which hid the pits like a smoke screen.

If Jack could escape, even for a short time, and get out at sea in a small boat, he might attract the naval plane's attention. But there would be another danger then, too. Other planes based here, which Fat Stuff had spoken of, could only be enemy planes. They would attack the patrol bomber. The reason no attack had been made on the bomber thus far was probably because the island was more valuable as an espionage base than as a base for air attack.

As Jack's mind centered on these thoughts, a whip cracked in the air behind him. Limehouse was approaching with an unpleasant gleam in his eye. Jack resumed his digging. The guard laughed.

"Much as I hate to interrupt the work you love so well," he began, "I must ask you to stop. The Head has asked me to bring you to his office. His wishes are most urgent."

Jack turned in his tools and followed Limehouse from the pit to a station wagon, which bumped him over the mountain road to the prison. A few minutes later the prisoner, covered with yellow dust, was escorted into an office in the administration building.

The dust-free air, the soft Oriental rug, the lavish furniture, all seemed to belong to a forgotten world of dreams.

"Wait here," Limehouse ordered, closing the door of the office.

Jack stood, silently waiting. A movement on the other side of the room caught his ears. He turned to see a figure rising from a chair—a girl with brown hair and soft,

To Jack's Surprise, a Plane Flew Over the Island

dreamy eyes.

"Betty!"

She had been facing the other way—she turned at the sound of Jack's voice. In spite of his shaved head and prison uniform, she recognized him.

"Powder!"

CHAPTER TEN

UNEXPECTED COMPLICATIONS

Instinctively the girl started toward him, then halted, her eyes wide with horror as the details of the change in him struck home.

"Powder!" she exclaimed. "Those convict stripes! Your hair! What has happened to you?"

Her question revealed her complete ignorance of the events since Jack had left her yacht. Betty's position in the spy ring had never been clear to Jack, and while all the evidence pointed to her being in league with The Head, he could never fully convince himself that she was heart and soul in that role.

The girl's actions now were too genuine to support the belief that she had been in The Head's confidence regarding the living doom of Death Rock. Nor had The Head told her "Powder" was here.

"The stripes and haircut mean that I'm now wholly within The Head's power," Jack announced. "I'm being held here because he regards me as a very dangerous enemy."

"Why should you be an enemy, Powder?" she asked. "I never could believe you were a spy—I don't believe you shot down Jim Roderick, The Head's pilot, in cold blood as The Head said you did. Yet you are in prison—"

"I shot Jim to keep him from killing me," Jack said. "He deserved it. Murder was a minor crime for him."

"Then it is true!"

"Why should you seem so shocked?" Jack asked. "Aren't you a spy yourself?"

"A spy? A spy against my own interests? Why, that is perfectly foolish!" Betty's eyes flashed indignantly. "Besides, my father runs his business on strictly ethical lines— while other firms may spy against him, he doesn't stoop that low!"

Suddenly Jack knew the truth. He knew now that Betty Brown, in calling Jack a spy, might not be speaking of the same kind of espionage that Jack referred to. The name "Brown" suddenly struck a familiar chord in Jack's memory.

"Betty," Jack asked suddenly, "are you the daughter of Old Man Brown—Isaac J. Brown—of South American Airlines?"

"Powder! Have you gone crazy? You worked for my father for years! You know who I am!"

That was it. Old Man Brown, fireball ace of the first World War, was almost a legendary figure in aviation. Jack slowly recalled that Brown did have a daughter. She was born in South America when Brown was starting his airline on a shoestring.

During the armistice years between the World Wars, Brown's aviation empire grew. There had been hints of Nazi backing, but no one believed that the cigar-chewing, gruff executive of the line could be "run" by anyone, even a pack of wolves like the Nazis.

But Jack was beginning to realize that somehow under cover operatives of Hitler's Nazi cohorts had wormed their way into Brown's confidence. They had used the line for their own ends, including possibly the transporting of shanghaied men to Death Rock. Unscrupulous pilots, men without countries, men loyal only to money, had been imported to work on the line. Powder and Jim had been of this type.

Perhaps Old Man Brown had been fooled by these men. Trusting implicitly in his executives, such as The Head probably was, he had allowed them free rein, not suspecting that they were using him as a blind for their own Fifth Column activities against the United Nations.

Jack recalled once that Betty had spoken of "the game" being in her blood. That her father had "been in the business fifteen years." Jack had thought she was referring to international spying and that Betty was the daughter of a spy. She had been talking about *aviation.*

The term "spy" as used by Betty did not refer to treacherous espionage against the United States, but to shady business methods. Many firms "spy" on other firms. Commercial spying is a highly paid profession, but not a criminal one.

Betty had not known the real activity in the Pacific that had resulted in the use of her yacht by The Head. Some trumped-up story had satisfied her, while the true objective was the theft of the American naval patrol plane.

"Listen, Betty!" Jack said. "If you'll only believe me, I can explain everything. But tell me one thing—why are you here?"

Betty looked deeply into Jack's eyes, searching for the answer to a question that was unspoken, yet clearly shown in her expression. She seemed puzzled, baffled, completely at a loss.

"Sometimes you don't act like the old Powder I used to know," she said. "You seem changed—a different man. I can't understand you—"

"I *am* a different man, Betty," Jack said. "I am not—"

Smilin' Jack suddenly checked himself. What was he saying? While The Head suspected that Jack was not really Powder, he had no real proof. Putting Betty alone in this room with Jack might be a trap. The Head undoubtedly sought to learn something by this ruse. Instead, Jack decided to tell something The Head might not want told.

"Listen, Betty," he said. "I am not a commercial spy. But The Head, who probably is a trusted official of your father's airline, is worse. He is an international spy, an enemy of our country. He tricked you into obtaining the use of your yacht to steal an American naval plane. Your father thinks The Head is working for you, but instead he is working for the Axis Powers—for the Nazis in particular."

A connecting door of the office swung open suddenly. In the doorway stood The Head, leveling an automatic pistol at Smilin' Jack. Behind the dwarfed little man was a huge, grotesque figure, The Claw, sharpening the hook on his right arm with a file.

"That's enough, *Mister* Powder!" snapped The Head.

The Claw crowded forward. He tossed the file aside and seized Jack by the coat, holding the hook menacingly in the air.

"Shall I give him the facial, Chief?" he asked. "I could do a better job than you could do with that popgun!"

"Let him alone, Claw!" The Head ordered.

He turned to Jack:

"My dear Powder," he began, "your assertions are ill-timed and ill-advised. I would suggest that you remember that you are completely in my power. Remember also that Miss Brown is now at my mercy. I own this island and the prison guards are quite obedient to my orders. True, some of the prisoners were convicted in the courts of a South American government, but that government is kept by my paid agent from being very curious about them or how they are treated here. Through my agents on the mainland I am able to alter penal records to conform to my purposes. It happens that some of these prisoners are women. Miss Brown might easily find herself among the forgotten convicts on this island—"

"You wouldn't dare!" Betty said defiantly, her eyes blazing.

The Head was expressionless. She turned to Jack.

"I'm beginning to understand, Powder. Strange, I never saw The Head in his true light before. Now I understand many things that struck me only as being odd. I realize why you were imprisoned aboard my yacht and why you are wearing stripes now." Then, to The Head, "My Father will kill you if you harm me, Mr. Ghindi!"

The Head smirked.

"Unfortunately, your father is not in a good position to do that," he said. "He is on the mainland many miles away. You are helpless here—any move he makes against me might result in your—ah—suffering. Should he try anything rash, he might suddenly find himself surrounded by men who are more loyal to me—for reasons they know best—than to the head of the firm that employs them."

Deep chagrin swept over Smilin' Jack. Instead of hampering The Head, as he had expected to do by telling Betty what sort of man he really was, Jack had jeopardized Betty's safety.

The Claw shifted uneasily as The Head threatened Betty.

"You ain't gonna hoit th' girl, are you, Chief?" he asked anxiously.

"Mind your own business, Claw!" The Head snapped.

"You'll never get away with this!" Jack told The Head. "You don't dare kidnap Betty Brown, as you've kidnaped me and the other poor devils held on Death Rock!"

The expression on The Head's face was as immobile

as the walls of his prison. Jack could not tell whether the threats against Betty were bluff or not.

"Miss Brown," The Head said, turning to the girl, "against my orders you went for a flight in the seaplane today."

Then it had been the seaplane, not a patrol plane, Jack and Fat Stuff had heard while working in the prison mine.

"And," The Head continued, "you saw a warship in waters off this island. Due to my foresight, the radio in the plane wasn't working, but you came back to your yacht to radio American authorities, because you recognized the warship as a Jap cruiser. Too bad, Miss Brown, but you now know too much. Put yourself in my position —if I allow you freedom you will ruin me. But I will not kill you, Miss Brown, because I owe your father so much for allowing me to use his business as a center for my espionage ring—although he was stupidly unaware of the fact."

"So that's why you told me I could notify authorities in prison of the warship and they would communicate with the American consul—"

"Yes, Miss Brown," the Head continued suavely. "I decided not to kill you. Your death would net me nothing. Besides, Mr. Trefwitz tells me we are short of women prisoners on this island. I shall notify your father that you have gone to visit friends in the United States for a time. Your disappearance will follow—and the assumption will be that your plane fell into the sea."

Jack restrained himself with difficulty. But he realized he could do nothing then—The Claw was too eager to use his hook on Jack, and The Head was too likely to pull the trigger of his automatic.

"You—you're a Nazi!" Betty gasped. "Only a Nazi could be so cruel!"

The Claw shifted uneasily on his feet, glancing anxiously at The Head and then at the girl. At last he spoke.

"Maybe we better not put the girl in the women's prison, Chief," he said. "It makes women old. She's pretty. She hasn't done nothing—"

"I'll decide, Claw. You need only *follow* my orders!" The Head spoke sharply. Then he turned to Betty. "Your opinion of me does not matter in the least. My actions are above the opinions of ordinary people."

"Isn't there something—anything—?" Betty began, and looked beseechingly at Jack. "Why couldn't you have told me before?"

"Powder—and I'm pretty well convinced this man is an impostor and not the real Powder we once knew— this man thought you were a spy, in league with us. While he would be unwilling to put you behind the bars of this prison, not so long ago he was working quite diligently to put you inside an American penitentiary."

"Who are you?" Betty asked Jack, in amazement.

"It does not matter who he is," The Head went on quickly. "But I think he can serve me. What do you think of having this lovely young woman sentenced for the remainder of her life on Death Rock?" he demanded

Betty Looked Beseechingly at Jack.

of Jack.

"It would be the most terrible crime you have ever committed," Jack said with cold fury in his voice.

"It is within your power to prevent it, Powder," The Head explained calmly. "Due to your rash actions and my own inefficiency and overconfidence I lost the new patrol bomber that my agents stole from the United States. Limehouse tells me that it sank in the lagoon at the other end of the island and the sea probably has torn it to pieces on the bottom of the lagoon by now. But I believe that if you communicated with your chief—the man who directs your spying—he would send a bomber to rescue you."

"I would be only too glad to let the United States know where I am," Jack said.

"You answer too quickly, Powder," The Head continued. "But you underestimate me if you think I was not prepared for that answer. No, your message will say nothing about this island. There is another island some distance from here where the bomber will land to 'rescue' you. When it arrives, the crew will be overpowered or slain, and I will have the plane. In return for this small favor, I will agree not to confine Miss Brown in the women's prison. Instead, she will live in a comfortable little cottage by the sea until the war is over."

Betty turned to Smilin' Jack and shook her head, to tell him to refuse.

"And you, Powder," The Head went on, "will be taken out of the sulphur mines until the period of your sentence is up."

"Do you think I would put any faith in your promises?" Jack asked. "How long do you think I'd live after you had your hands on the patrol bomber?"

"How long do you think you'll live in the sulphur mines, with your lungs encrusted with yellow dust?" The Head asked.

"I would live longer than I would with my spine tinted yellow!" Jack returned angrily.

"And you will leave this sweet, lovely American girl to rot in the Death Rock prison laundry?"

"I won't rot and I won't be in your prison long," Betty said. "You won't get away with this as easily as you think."

"I will give you one last chance, Powder!" The Head said, his cold eyes resting on Smilin' Jack's face. "What is your decision? Will you follow my orders?"

"I'll answer for him! He won't!" Betty exclaimed hotly.

The Head still was looking at Jack. He disregarded the girl's reply.

Jack turned toward Betty. To think of her lovely face streaked with agony, her fingers cracked from working over steaming washing machines—

"Hurry! Make your decision!" The Head urged.

On the other hand, if the enemy copied the American bomber, cities in the United States would be bombed. Thousands of girls like Betty Brown would be torn and twisted in death—

"Go jump in the ocean!" Jack said finally.

"My, my! Your friend certainly isn't the one for gallantry!" The Head taunted Betty. "He'll trade you for a bomber any day."

"If he hadn't, I'd have as low an opinion of him as I now have of you!" Betty declared.

"And he'll suffer because he has! Back to the mines for you, Powder. And as for you, Miss Brown—Claw, take her to the prison laundry."

The huge, one-armed giant hesitated. His bestial eyes blinked a dim-witted revolt. His twisted nose twitched in distaste for his job.

Then, so surprisingly that it startled friend and foe alike, tears ran down his cheeks and his voice exploded with a sob:

. "I—I j-j-just c-c-can't d-d-do it, Chief" The Claw cried. "She-she's s-s-so p-p-pretty! I j-j-just c-c-can't."

As the bullet-headed beast began to weep, The Head's expression showed fury—the first violent emotion Smilin' Jack had ever observed on the usually motionless features. A purple rage swept from brow to chin. The dwarf's hands clenched and unclenched as he sought to control himself in the face of this rebellion in the man who had once obeyed his smallest command.

"Do you know what it means to refuse me, Claw?" The Head thundered in hoarse rage. "Do as I say!"

"I—I c-c-can't!" sobbed the Claw.

"For the last time—"

"K-K-Kill m-m-me, Chief. But I—I c-c-can't!"

The Head's eyes burned as he glowered at the blubbering giant. Then, somehow, he seemed to regain control of himself. His face grew calm, as before. A dangerous expression shot into his eyes. Smilin' Jack felt sorry for the moronic giant who cried like a schoolboy at the thought of destroying beauty.

The Head stepped forward. Quick as a flash, he seized The Claw's right arm. He twisted suddenly, and the hook came loose from the leather covering on the stump and fell to the floor.

"Limehouse!" The Head called.

The door swung open and the ugly face of the guard appeared. As Limehouse's eyes took in the scene, he seemed to understand what had happened. Smilin' Jack and Betty, both pale, stood straight and determined. The Claw, disarmed of his sharp hook, had slumped into a chair where he sat with tears running down his cheeks.

The Head turned to The Claw.

"No, Claw, I won't kill you. After all, you have done me many favors and I shall reward you by letting you live. You may have a chance later to win your freedom. I'll let you think over your disobedience in the sulphur mines, working at Powder's side."

Limehouse came further into the room, a look of expectancy on his sleek face.

"Yes, Chief?" he asked.

"Send Miss Brown to the prison laundry to be dressed-in," The Head ordered. "The Claw is to be dressed-in also, at the men's prison. Powder is to be taken back to the mines."

Limehouse's eyes danced as he snapped handcuffs on The Claw's wrist. The Head's chief lieutenant had fallen from favor, and it was easy to see that Limehouse coveted the post.

Limehouse snapped a second cuff to Jack and then prodded the two toward the door, where he was met by a matron from the women's prison who had been summoned to escort Betty to a cell.

As Jack and The Claw were escorted through the courtyard to the station wagon which was to take them to the receiving gate of the mine, the tears ceased streaming from the giant's eyes and a sullen look of hatred spread over his countenance.

"After all I've done for him, he asks me to do that to a lady!" The Claw muttered. "I'm a gentleman, I am. I don't mistreat no dames!"

CHAPTER ELEVEN

THE SELF-APPOINTED BOSS

With ironic justice The Claw was locked with the other prisoners in the bull pen that night. Jack wondered whether such disloyalty to The Head as that displayed by The Claw was a permanent thing. Perhaps The Claw would now be on Jack's side. His low mentality made him of small value in formulating plans to escape, but where brawn and brute courage were needed, The Claw might come in extremely handy—as an ally.

Yet Jack hesitated to trust this misshapen monster of a man. The influence The Head had exerted over The Claw might be so deeply instilled in the brute that any action on Jack's part to divert him to other purposes might drive him back to The Head. It would not be wise to rely on him too heavily, but Jack still might find him useful.

In Fat Stuff, of course, Jack had someone he could fully trust. That loyal soul was incapable of scheming against a friend.

"There's a new girl prisoner, Fat Stuff," Jack revealed as they lay on the board that served them for a bed in the bull pen.

"Um? Pretty girl not stay pretty very long here," the native said.

"We've got to get out—and get her out!" Jack declared, vehemently.

"Um! New prisoner Jack's sweetheart, maybe?"

"No, Fat Stuff," Jack said with a shake of his head, "but Betty—that's the girl's name—saved my life once and here's my chance to repay her. If we can escape, we'll see that she gets away, too."

"You havum plan to escape now, Jack?" Fat Stuff asked practically.

"I'm working on something, but I'll need your help."

"You work on something; I work on something; everybody work on something, but nobody escapes," Fat Stuff said simply. "Me think hard at night while I sleep, but no better think come out than when I wake up."

Through the days that followed, while The Claw adjusted himself with the resignation of an animal to the man-killing routine, Smilin' Jack proceeded carefully to impress upon the one-armed man that "Powder" was trying to be his friend. He did this by performing small services. Slowly these little favors began to have their effect, and Jack noted that the other convicts made no more attempts to play their vengeful little tricks while The Claw was around.

During this time, while other convicts slept at night, Jack was busy, working with two bits of metal on the concrete floor of the bull-pen. At last, three days after The Claw had been sent to the sulphur mines with Jack, the plan for escape was ready to put into execution.

It was dusk, with the day's work finished. Convicts

coughing the yellow dust from their lungs, were allowed a few minutes relaxation before retiring. In this period
the men were allowed to converse in the big enclosure,
and they seized this opportunity for passing news from
man to man.

Tonight, Jack moved to one end of the bull pen. The
guards were far away, out of earshot.

"I've got something to say to you boys," Jack suddenly
announced to the men near him.

Startled expressions crossed the faces of the convicts.
Powder, the most unpopular man in the whole prison,
was addressing the others as equals. Lizard guffawed and
nudged Slab.

"Shut up, Lizard!" Jack said quietly, but with author-
ity in his tone.

Lizard swung around and faced Jack sullenly.

"Who do ya t'ink ya are?" he asked. "I can laugh if I
wanna."

"Not while I have something to say," Jack declared.

Knowing that only an overbearing manner would be
effective, Jack abandoned his usual good-natured disposition. Stern insistence upon discipline was understood
by these men, bullied by guards and mistreated as an
everyday experience.

"Just what have *you* got to say?" Slab asked, backing
up his partner, Lizard.

"I was about to announce that there are going to be
some changes around here," Jack said, looking squarely
at the two convicts. "The Head and Limehouse may run

the prison on the surface, but I intend to run it on the inside."

"Huh?"

Jack's brazen announcement, made with deliberate calm, caught the prisoners off balance.

"Now if there's any objections from some of you boys," Jack continued, surveying the group with cold calculation, "I'm willing to argue. But before anyone gets rash, I'd like to point out that I'm fairly handy with my fists— and Fat Stuff isn't all fat, but he has quite a bit of muscle. Besides, I've got another friend here—the man you know as The Claw."

All eyes turned toward The Claw, a miserable newcomer in their midst. Although The Claw had been closely associated with The Head, he was unknown to the prisoners. The Claw, whose duties were those of bodyguard for The Head, had not been seen inside the prison often enough to be recognized as a former lieutenant of the man at the top.

But The Claw was not the formidable figure he once had been. His iron hook—the weapon that lent a vicious touch to the giant's ferocious manner—was gone. The Claw, seated on the floor, was weeping.

"Ho, ho!" Lizard laughed, recovering from the first shock of Jack's announcement. "Looky! Who's afraid of dat big slob! Th' baby's bawlin'!"

Slab reached out, seized Jack by the coat and drew him close, the black eyes of the convict's distorted face burning into Jack's. Slab raised his fist menacingly.

The Claw, Seated on the Floor, Was Weeping

"Why, you fresh guy!" Slab roared. "Who do you t'ink you are—tellin' us you're gonna be de big shot here?"

"Yeah!" Lizard echoed, stepping close to Slab. "If th' screws wasn't so clost, we'd take a poke at ya! Tryin' to scare us with a big slob of a cry baby!"

Jack deliberately raised his foot and stamped down on Slab's toes.

"OW!"

The convict emitted a gasp of pain and released his hold on Jack.

Slab closed in, but as Jack stepped back, his cold eyes met those of the convict. Uncertain what to do, Slab hesitated.

"Not so fast!" Jack said. "The Claw hasn't been in his right mind since a friend of his let him down. Besides, he isn't quite all there. Limehouse took an important part of his character when he removed the hook he used to have on his right arm."

It hadn't been Limehouse who had removed The Claw's hook, but Jack believed it best not to stress The Claw's prior association with the hated operator of the prison mine.

"He still don't scare me," Slab said, trying to get up enough courage to tackle Jack in an exchange of blows.

"I think, with the proper accessories, The Claw can be quite frightening, even to such men as you, Slab," Jack announced with a half-smile.

Reaching beneath the board that served as Jack's bed, the aviator withdrew two pieces of metal—one a sharp spear and the other a saw-like blade with a sharp edge. During the nights while other convicts slept, Smilin' Jack had filed them from a chisel and a spoon by rubbing them on the concrete floor of his cell.

"These may be crude instruments," Jack went on, "but they're sharp and they fit The Claw's socket perfectly."

Smilin' Jack turned and thrust the saw-like blade into the socket on the leather covering fixed to the stump of The Claw's right arm. At the sight of the blade where his old hook had been, a transformation took place in the blubbering face of the giant. Tears vanished and his eyes glistened with happiness. The Claw's crooked mouth widened into a grin of unholy glee as he became master of himself once again.

Jack watched, uncertain what reaction might take place. Would The Claw show loyalty to Jack, who had fashioned him a new weapon for his crippled arm, or would The Claw's dull mind revert to habitual subjugation to The Head?

Rising sullenly to his feet, The Claw turned his eyes on the circle of convicts, as if he awaited an opportunity to spring on one of them. The prisoners moved back, murmuring uneasily.

"Call him off, Powder!" Slab pleaded.

Others echoed the plea, and The Claw turned to Jack.

"You want me to fix 'em, Powder?" he asked.

Jack shook his head in negation.

"Not now," he said. Then he addressed the group: "I'm The Claw's friend because I've restored his self-confidence. He's my loyal partner now. Is there any man who still doubts who's running this show?"

As Jack spoke, The Claw moved his jagged weapon in an arc toward the shrinking convicts.

"None here, *boss!*" Slab croaked hoarsely.

"You're *It,* far as I'm concerned," muttered Lizard abjectly.

"Okay!" echoed another voice. "You're the big shot."

Jack surveyed the mob of hardened men with a smile. The first part of his plan had succeeded. By capitalizing on the strength of The Claw and by using his own wits, Smilin' Jack had welded these beaten men into a semblance of unity. These men were tough and as long as Jack had The Claw and Fat Stuff to back him up, he could lead them. Jack had a plan—an idea suggested to him on his trips from the cell-house to the mine when he occasionally caught glimpses of brilliantly plumed birds on the island.

"Move around and pretend not to be listening to me while I explain my plan," Jack said. "The boys at the other end of the bull pen are making enough noise to keep the guards from hearing what I say."

Jack was not afraid of the guards. He had waited for a time when a certain pair of guards were on duty. These two, he felt, might be bribed, and he was counting on their help on his plan. Already Jack had hinted to these men that they might earn some "easy money." He had promised them a "cut" from a "graft" from the outside if these two guards "played ball." The guards were "playing ball" now by allowing Jack and his fellow convicts to converse without being overheard.

"What're you up to, Powder?" Slab asked.

"Now we're gettin' down to business," Jack said. "The thing I'm thinking about is what every man here is thinking about! *Escape!*"

Jack barely whispered the word, but the stir among the convicts indicated that all had heard it.

"The most essential thing is money!" Jack announced, glancing around at the prisoners for the reaction he expected.

It came.

"You're right, Powder," Slab said, "but money don't grow on leg irons!"

"True and wisely spoken, Slab," Jack replied, as though approving Slab's wisecrack. "But money does grow on this island. It grows on tropical birds and I know how to pick it. Boys, we're going to *feather* our nest!"

Slab's piggish eyes glinted with a new admiration for the man he knew as "Powder."

"*Feather?*" he asked.

"Right!" Jack said with a nod. "That's the exact word for what we're going to do. Many of the beautiful birds that inhabit this island paradise—" he paused and grinned as he noticed the sour looks of his fellow prisoners, "—perhaps I should simply say 'island'—have valuable plumage, much sought by importers in the United States."

"Hm-m-m!"

Slab and the other prisoners were thinking. Whether the idea sounded crazy or not, it had an angle. These men were desperate, willing to gamble on anything that afforded hope of escape.

"We'll catch the birds," Jack continued. "I'll buy the feathers of the birds you catch. I think I've spotted a guard who, for a cut of the profits, will deliver them to a man on the outside who'll pay a fair price for our industry."

"There's just one catch in the idea," Lizard said. "How're we gonna catch the birds when we're in a cage ourselves?"

Smilin' Jack laughed.

"Quite simply," he explained. "We can bribe certain guards to let us pluck birds as we go to and from timber camps and the sulphur mines. I've been watching these guards and they're not above a little easy dough. They couldn't be and work for a shanghai joint like Death Rock!"

Slab was scratching his hairless head. Lizard was stroking his chin. All of the convicts within earshot were thinking deeply.

"It may be a disgrace to me perfession," said one of the convicts. "I've robbed everyt'ing from delicatessens to armored trucks, but stealin' tail feathers from boids ain't beneat' me, if there's a chance in it to bust outa here."

A mumbled cheer indicated others were willing to

gamble also.

"Okay, boys," Jack said. "I think I can make arrangements with the 'screws' to start work tomorrow. Remember—the guy that squawks will have to explain to The Claw!"

"Nobody's gonna squawk," Slab said. "We'll see to that."

"Say, Powder!" Lizard blurted out, "we been treatin' you plenty dirty—an' maybe you deserve it—but get us out of here an' everyt'ing's square."

"I'll do my best," Jack promised.

As the convicts drifted away to discuss the plan in small groups, Smilin' Jack sought out Fat Stuff. Whether the plan afforded a good chance to escape or not, Jack was sure of one thing—he no longer had to fear that these men would try to get even with the man they knew as Powder.

Fat Stuff saw a good chance to obtain further loyalty from the men unjustly and cruelly imprisoned at Death Rock.

"Why not ask Claw to tell others you not Powder?" he asked.

Jack considered the idea and then shook his head.

"The Claw isn't quite right in his head, Fat Stuff," Jack said. "He's not very smart—my real identity means nothing to him. In fact, I doubt if the big ox fully realizes that I'm not Powder Pellet."

"Well," Fat Stuff decided, "me gonna try to catch birds so we get plenty money for escape."

Jack had hopes for the ultimate success of his extraordinary plan, but even the cleverest of plans to escape would have long odds against it in this prison. But once Jack had his chance, he would play it to the limit and he would try his best to free Betty Brown at the same time from the women's prison on the island.

"Say, Fat Stuff," Jack asked, "where is the women's prison located?"

Fat Stuff understood.

"Thinkum about pretty girl Betty, eh?" he asked. "Woman prison on separate island—Devil Kitchen—just off coast of Death Rock. Me there once."

"Why were *you* there?"

"Cells for solitary confinement also on that island," Fat Stuff said.

A cell door clanged and a hoarse voice shouted: "Break it up!"

Jack turned and saw the satanic features of Limehouse, who was just entering the bull pen. For an instant Jack was alarmed. What if Limehouse had some secret listening device concealed so that he had overheard Jack's plan to raise funds for a prison break?

But Limehouse seemed to pay no attention to Jack or to any special prisoner. Limehouse had entered the bull pen simply for "amusement." The guard seemed to enjoy visiting the unhappy convicts, bullying them in their helplessness. There walked a perfect Nazi, a born Gestapo henchman, Jack thought grimly. Adolf Hitler's Storm Troopers were just of such pitiless mold.

As he moved across the pen, one of the convicts, a man known as Eagle Eye, failed to hear his approach. Limehouse swung his foot and kicked the man roughly out of the way.

Eagle Eye turned around, fire blazing in his eyes.

"Guard or no guard," he said coldly, "you kick me like that again, Limehouse, an' you'll be sorry."

Limehouse's smug smile did not change.

"So?" he asked. "Well, I'm curious, Eagle Eye. Let's just see what you'll do to make me sorry."

As he spoke, the prison guard swung his foot, catching Eagle Eye on the side of his hip, knocking the unfortunate prisoner back against the bars of the pen. The brutal blow was the typical kind of heartless cruelty that Limehouse enjoyed. He practiced his little malevolences with impunity, for no one dared report him to higher officials of the prison—who perhaps would not have interfered anyway.

For a second Eagle Eye crouched where he had fallen, glaring up at Limehouse, who was laughing tauntingly at the helpless man, confident that the convict had no chance to do him harm. His was a coward's courage.

Then Eagle Eye sprang. With the speed of a striking serpent he launched a wicked blow from his shoe-tops. Limehouse tried to protect himself, but the attack was so swift he had no time. The prisoner's fist caught him on the tip of his pointed chin, jerking his head back and dropping him to the floor with a thump.

A cry of unholy glee rose from the prisoners. As Limehouse landed in a limp sprawl, twitched once, and then lay motionless. Shouts of dismay came from the other guards. The convicts backed away and stood in sullen, muttering groups.

A bell jangled. Guards streamed into the bull pen with whips and guns to quell what seemed to be a riot. Eagle Eye was buried under a pile of guards who pounced on him unmercifully. Quickly Limehouse was carried out to be revived.

"Wow!" Smilin' Jack whispered to Fat Stuff. "At last Limehouse got a dose of what was coming to him. I surely wish we had that man Eagle Eye in our organization. He'd help us no end."

Fat Stuff shook his head dejectedly.

"We never see Eagle Eye again," he said with a solemn sigh.

"Why, what'll they do to him?" Jack asked.

"Mebbe givum year in dungeon, or solitary—one bad as other worse. If Limehouse neck brokum, Eagle Eye get guillotine—but he no such lucky."

This information had a sobering effect on Smilin' Jack, as he realized that the minor atrocities piled upon the prisoners by the guards would have only one effect on a normal, red-blooded man. Sooner or later a man with courage would rebel against constant heckling. Eagle Eye's actions and fate might someday be Jack's own. Jack had to escape before he was placed in an escape-proof dungeon!

There was more than Jack's own future at stake. There

was a gigantic spy ring operating against the United States that could be smashed once Jack was free to notify authorities at home. And then there was—Betty.

Nothing must stand in the way of Jack's escape.

CHAPTER TWELVE

A BREAK FOR FREEDOM

In his appraisal of the prison guards, Jack was uncannily accurate. Most of them were the scum of humanity, picked up in the cesspools of humanity by The Head to perform his lowest deeds. One or two of them had been prisoners themselves, shanghaied to the island by underlings of The Head and then given posts to guard other unfortunates after they had completed their unjust terms. Their lot was not much better, and they could be tempted easily by any promise of gold.

With the explanation of riches to come from plumes of island birds, Jack found several guards willing to aid him. These guards accepted feathers collected by the convicts, and, since they themselves lacked the intelligence and organizing ability to carry on the business without Jack's help, they quickly accorded the American aviator privileges that gave him time to make plans for escape.

Limehouse's injury at the hands of Eagle Eye aided Jack, for it was doubtful if Limehouse, had he been present, would have permitted Jack some of the privileges he got. Limehouse seemed to have a personal hatred for Smilin' Jack—or rather, "Powder"—and Jack assumed this was in retaliation for fancied wrongs Limehouse had endured at the hands of Powder in the past. Perhaps the unfound treasure had something to do with it.

But Limehouse had suffered a slight concussion from the blow landed by Eagle Eye and the prison guard was confined to the hospital while Jack and his fellow convicts were exchanging plumes of tropical birds for privileges in the bull pen.

During this time Jack worked under cover, examining the locks and automatic guarding devices of the prison. The gates of the big pen were operated by electricity from a central control station in the cell block. To prevent the complete locking of the doors, it was only necessary for Jack to adjust the motor mechanism so that the doors were partly closed, instead of shut completely.

A single guard barred the way to freedom once the convicts made their way past the doors of the bull pen. He carried keys that would unlock outer doors. Then the main gate could be rushed.

A liberal collection of feathers—meaning greater spoils to divide—would make guards outside the cell blocks less observant of what went on.

With the plans formulated, Jack called his fellow unfortunates together. Every convict was assigned a task. Fat Stuff, familiar with the island, would act as a guide through the jungle. Slab and Lizard would overpower the guard in the bull pen. Out of the twenty convicts in the block, most of them should get away—and the odds were not too great that all would escape.

But The Claw received the news of escape quite differently from what Jack expected.

"We gotta get the girl out too," he said.

"The girl?" Jack asked.

"Yes, Betty Brown. Unless she goes, I not go."

"Listen," Jack said. "No one wants to get Betty out of prison more than I do, but we can't take the risk now. Once we are free, I know I can spring her from the outside and put The Head and his gang in prison in our places. But we've got to get away ourselves first."

"Then I stay!" The Claw announced decisively.

Jack needed The Claw. He was not so sure that as Powder he would be safe among the other convicts without the protection of the huge one-armed giant.

Suddenly Jack had an idea. His hand slipped under the board used by The Claw for a bed. In a second he had the two sharp tools he had fashioned for The Claw's arm socket concealed under his coat.

"All right," Jack said. "You can stay. Maybe you can get Betty out yourself, from the inside."

"No," The Claw announced. "If you go, I go, but I'll stop at the women's cell-house and get Betty out."

"How?" Jack asked, watching The Claw closely.

The giant smiled and reached under his board bed. Jack watched him closely. A look of dismay crossed The Claw's face as he found his substitute "claws" missing.

"They're gone!" he whispered hoarsely. Tears began to well into his eyes. "They're gone! Without them, I'm no good!"

"You can have them again, Claw," Jack said.

"You know where they are?" The Claw's eyes flashed and his left hand moved toward Jack.

For a moment Jack expected an attack, but he stood his ground. His gray eyes flashed into the dim eyes of the giant. For a second The Claw hesitated, his self-confidence gone without his "claw." In that hesitation, The Claw lost.

"Well?" Jack asked. "Do you go with us?"

Slowly The Claw nodded.

"I go, but I come back for the girl," he said, with a crafty look in his eyes.

When Jack left The Claw that night, he felt gravely uncertain that he could trust the man. But to try to escape without him would be suicide, for hatreds still smoldered among the prisoners for the man who had stolen the freedom of so many.

Jack managed to "doctor" the cell lock mechanism and everything was prepared. It was a long chance, but the only one. Limehouse would be out of the hospital before long—and then opportunity for escape would be gone.

Through the day, the men worked silently in the sulphur mines. The very quietness of the prisoners should have aroused suspicion among the guards, but these men were not conscientious overseers.

At night the men were led back to the cell block. Jack no longer had to go without his night meal, which had been taken away by Limehouse as punishment for his fight with Lizard. But tomorrow he would be free and he could eat to his heart's content of the fruit and berries that abounded in the jungle.

The "lights out" warning came at last. The convicts settled back on their boards, listening to the footsteps of the guards outside the cells. Not one of the guards suspected that the doors of the cell-houses were not completely locked.

Time wore on. The guards ceased their stealthy patrol. Slowly Jack rose from his bunk. He tried the door. It slid back. He stepped out into the bull pen. Along the tier of cells other doors opened and silent figures dressed in stripes emerged.

At the end of the big enclosure was a guard—sleeping. Lizard and Slab crept forward.

A dull thud came to Jack's ears. He felt no pity for the guard, dozing at his post. This guard, like many of the others, had often indulged in petty cruelties to torment the prisoners: he got his deserts.

Lizard returned and pressed some keys into Jack's hand.

"Follow me!" Jack whispered.

A few minutes later the group of convicts reached the court. They followed shadows, keeping out of sight of the beams of searchlights that lighted the prison yard.

They reached the gate. Jack pulled back the bolts and pressed forward.

The gate was locked!

A groan came softly from the other convicts.

"We're not stumped yet, boys!" Jack said.

He felt underneath his coat. The jagged, saw-edged blade he had made for The Claw was there.

"Come here, Claw!" Jack said.

The burly giant stepped forward.

"Here's your claw for being a good boy. Do you think you can pick the lock with it?"

"Sure!" The Claw said, beaming as he felt the weapon in the socket of his artificial wrist once more.

Huddled in the shadow of the wall, The Claw inserted the rude prong into the keyhole. The scraping of metal came audibly to Jack's ears, but apparently the sound was too faint to be heard by the guards on the walls. There was a muffled *click*.

"There!" cried The Claw hoarsely.

The gate swung open.

"Make a break for it, boys!" Jack shouted. "Don't all go in the same direction!"

The convicts streamed through the gate.

One man stumbled into the path of a searchlight beam. A startled cry sounded on the wall. A rifle cracked and the convict fell forward on the ground.

A siren began to wail on the wall. The escape had been discovered!

But Jack and Fat Stuff were well out of the gate by now.

"Follow me!" the native called to Jack.

They plunged into the underbrush and made their way down the steep side of the mountain toward the sea.

Someone was following. Jack turned to see three figures bobbing in the darkness behind him. They were gaining, but there were no commands to halt. These men were convicts too, not guards.

After stumbling down the steep sides of the hill, they reached the beach. Fat Stuff led the way along the sand until they reached the section that was thickly covered with jungle.

"We pretty safe here," Fat Stuff announced, puffing. "We rest."

Jack sat down and the three other convicts joined them. They were The Claw, Lizard and Slab.

The situation in which Jack now found himself was not altogether to his liking. It was going to be three against two.

"When we go back to get Betty?" The Claw asked as he sat down beside Jack.

"I told you, Claw, that Betty will be released from the prison, but we're not in the clear yet ourselves," Jack said.

A non-committal grunt came from the giant.

As they rested they heard distant cries and shouts, and then they faintly heard the baying of bloodhounds. The pursuit of the escaped prisoners was on.

"Can we get away from them?" Jack asked Fat Stuff.

"Island pretty big," the native said. "We follow river near here—gettum bloodhounds off scent."

"Let's get goin'!" Slab suggested.

All that night the escaped prisoners made their way through the jungle. Thorny vines plucked at their clothing and their legs grew tired, but the baying of the distant bloodhounds kept them moving.

At last Fat Stuff brought them to the bank of a small stream that flowed from the hills through the jungles to the sea. They stepped into the cool, refreshing water and followed it upstream for half a mile before stepping out on the bank on the other side.

From there on the sound of pursuit grew fainter. By morning they had reached a spot deep in the interior of the island.

Here they sat down to rest, at last.

"How're we gonna get off this island?" Slab asked. "We ain't got a boat."

"There are natives at the south end with outrigger canoes," Jack said. "The canoes are small, but there have been a number of remarkable journeys made in them. In fact, natives covered the whole Pacific in those canoes before the white man came."

Slab rose to his feet and walked toward some berries growing on a vine near by.

"I'm dyin' of hunger," Slab said. "I'm gonna eat some of these berries."

But Fat Stuff ran forward and caught Slab's arm before the sunken-faced man had a chance to pick them.

"No, Slab!" the native cried. "No eat! Poison!"

Slab sat down with the rest, his eyes still fixed hungrily on the berries.

For awhile they slept. Then they arose and prepared to march southward to the native settlement.

Slab found some fruit before they had gone half a mile and he plucked it joyfully. Again Fat Stuff stopped him with the warning that it, too, was poison.

The jungle seemed to have berries and luscious fruit on every tree, but each time Slab sought to eat some, Fat Stuff stopped him with the warning:

"No eat, Slab. Poison."

At last Slab spotted some purple grapes on a vine that ran up a tree.

"There's stuff I *know* ain't poison!" he said. "Them's grapes."

"No eat, Slab! Poison!" Fat Stuff warned again.

Lizard turned accusingly toward the native.

"Say!" he growled. "I think you're tryin' to starve us, Fat Stuff! You and Powder want to give th' rest of us th' slip an' get away without us. You say every fruit we see is poison."

"Yeah!" Slab growled. "You can't fool me no longer!"

With a vicious shove, Slab pushed Fat Stuff aside and plucked the grapes. He thrust them piggishly into his mouth and gulped them down.

"No! No eat! Poison!" Fat Stuff cried, rushing toward Slab.

Again the escaped prisoner thrust the native aside.

He devoured another bunch of the grapes, and started on a third, when he hesitated.

"I feel kinda funny!" he said, staggering.

Slab tried to catch himself on the trunk of a tree, but he slipped and fell. A moment later he writhed and then

Fat Stuff Led the Way Through the Jungle

lay still as the others tried in vain to revive him.

Jack bent over the still figure and felt his pulse. He listened to his chest, then moved away.

"Fat Stuff was right," Jack said. "Those grapes were poison. Quick, too. Slab is dead."

"Me try stop him," Fat Stuff said apologetically.

"It was his own fault," Lizard said coldly. He turned to Fat Stuff. "Lead us outa this blasted jungle. Find us some food that ain't poison!"

"Ugh!" growled The Claw. "Hurry. Me hungry."

The Claw and Lizard were going mad from hunger, but Jack felt safter now. Neither of the other two would try anything as long as only Fat Stuff knew which food to eat. And they found no berries or fruit that were edible as they went on through the jungle.

All that day they made their way slowly and painfully southward. At nightfall Fat Stuff found a bush with a few plum-like objects hanging from the branches.

"We eat this fruit," Fat Stuff announced. "Me know this fruit is not poison."

There were only two apiece for the hungry men.

On the morning of the third day they set out once more. They felt reasonably certain now that they had eluded the bloodhounds, but the menace of hunger grew. Edible fruit was scarce in the jungle. When bushes of wholesome berries were found there was barely enough to go around.

The Claw and Lizard were growing weak, while Jack was barely able to keep his legs moving. Fat Stuff's reserve seemed greater than the others, but even he devoured food eagerly whenever he found it.

Toward noon of the third day they reached another stream. Jack plunged in, leading the party toward the opposite bank. But as he made a second step, something caught him by the ankle and held him fast.

As Jack struggled to break away from what was holding him, his other foot was caught. The more he struggled the deeper he sank.

Jack was horrified at the realization of what had befallen him.

"Help!" Jack gasped as the water reached his armpits. "Quicksand!"

Fat Stuff ran toward the bank of the river ready to plunge into the water to help Jack.

Suddenly there was a growl and The Claw stepped forward, blocking the native's path.

"Let me past!" Fat Stuff cried. "Me gotta save my friend!"

The Claw brandished the knife-like weapon on the stump of his arm.

"How'd you like to have me puncture that fat body of yours?" he asked. "There's too many of us now! There'll be more to eat after we get rid of Powder!"

"Yeah! Let him go!" Lizard said. "I never did get even with him for tossin' me into that prison! Now I can watch him die!"

After shoving Fat Stuff aside, The Claw stood beside Lizard on the bank of the stream, while Jack slowly sank in the treacherous sand. The water reached Jack's chin and was crawling higher.

Absorbed in the struggles of the man they knew as Powder, The Claw and Lizard failed to notice Fat Stuff slip away.

The water reached Jack's mouth. In a moment it would be over his nostrils. Grimly and stoically Jack faced his fate.

But Fat Stuff was not giving up. He had climbed a near-by tree and from a limb he was lowering vines to Jack, helplessly caught by the sucking sand.

The Claw spotted the native as the vine was lowered to Jack. The aviator caught the vine and began slowly to pull himself up, out of the grip of the quicksand.

Lizard shrieked with anger as he saw that Jack was about to escape. The Claw's massive left arm swept upward and caught a limb of a near-by tree. The limb snapped and the giant tore it loose. Then he swung the long pole toward the vine.

The stick landed with a *whack* across Smilin' Jack's straining knuckles.

CHAPTER THIRTEEN

A JUNGLE VILLAGE

Vindictively, furiously, The Claw brought the branch down across Smilin' Jack's knuckles again and again as the aviator gripped the vines grimly, trying to pull himself out of the quicksand. Lizard jumped up and down on the bank, screaming with excitement.

The pain in his fingers was severe, but Jack held on desperately. He felt his feet pulling loose from the mire —a few more tugs and he would be free of the sand—if he could keep his hold despite The Claw's smarting blows from the pole.

The Claw viciously whacked at Jack's knuckles, but suddenly the attack ceased. A brown-skinned figure came zooming out of a near-by tree, swinging on a low hanging vine.

It was the South Sea Islander. He skimmed straight toward the two men on the bank of the stream. His feet struck like twin battering rams, bowling Lizard and The Claw to the ground like tenpins.

Exerting his final ounce of strength, Jack drew himself free of the quicksand. Using the vines for support, he dragged himself to the opposite bank of the stream.

"Come on, Fat Stuff!" he cried.

Fat Stuff, chortling with glee at Jack's escape and his

successful surprise attack on the two who had sought to get rid of Jack, swung across the stream on his vine.

"Follow me!" Fat Stuff said, plunging into the jungle with Jack at his heels. "We lose 'em."

But Lizard already was on his feet. Instantly he caught the swinging vine that Fat Stuff had dropped. Quickly he swung across the stream, shouting for The Claw to join him.

"Can't let 'em get away!" Lizard cried. "That native bloke is the only guy as can get us out of this jungle!"

The Claw, badly jarred from the punch of Fat Stuff's naked heels, rose painfully and seized the vine. He swung himself across the stream and trotted doggedly after Lizard.

Jack and Fat Stuff, aware of the pursuit, were trying to increase the distance between themselves and their treacherous companions. Fat Stuff's pace was slackening, however, as his huge body began to demand rest from his exertions.

"Hurry!" Jack urged. "Keep going! They're gaining on us."

"Fat Stuff—too fat!" the native panted. "No can—run fast."

Alone, Jack might have outdistanced them, but he couldn't desert this faithful follower now. Jack seized Fat Stuff's arm and tried to hurry him along, but the islander shook his head.

"No use, Jack!" he said. "Go on. Me can't go. Look like—me in—for much trouble."

"If *you're* in for it, we're *both* in for it," Jack insisted. "I'll stick by you, Fat Stuff, because you've stuck by me."

In a spurt of his second wind, Jack dragged the native into some brush which looked like a good hiding place. He had to conserve his energy now if he was going to meet and oppose The Claw and Lizard, both half-crazy from hunger and bitterly seeking revenge.

The two double-crossing pursuers came into view.

"They're in the brush!" Lizard shouted, spying the swaying vines where Jack and Fat Stuff had crawled to cover.

The Claw brandished the jagged blade on his arm. His eyes rolled with villainous intent.

"No use," cried Fat Stuff. "They find us!"

But Jack said, "You take Lizard. I'll handle The Claw!"

As Jack's head rose above the undergrowth, The Claw bellowed like a maddened bull. On spotting the aviator his bloodshot eyes actually saw red.

Fat Stuff instinctively shrank back as the two convicts came toward them, but Jack stubbornly stood his ground.

Something compelling in Jack's attitude caused The Claw to change his course—to attack Fat Stuff instead of the determined American. But as the Claw dived for Fat Stuff, Smilin' Jack went into action with a flying tackle.

The aim was sure. Jack's lunge caught The Claw just as he charged on Fat Stuff. The tackle threw The Claw to the ground, but it didn't knock him out. As Jack sprang forward to land a knockout blow, The Claw—on his back—kicked hard, his huge feet catching Jack on the chest and sending him staggering back.

With the wind knocked from his lungs, Jack gasped for breath. The Claw sprang to his feet and closed in toward Fat Stuff.

"Wait, you dope!" Lizard shouted from behind the giant idiot. "Don't bump off our guide!"

Reluctantly, The Claw turned toward Jack.

"There! That's the ticket!" Lizard shouted approvingly. "Anythin' you do to Powder is okay by me!"

By now Fat Stuff had his fright under control. When he saw The Claw going after his friend, he leaped to the fray. With his head down, Fat Stuff charged like a steamroller straight at the great bulk of The Claw.

The Lizard sprang like lightning into Fat Stuff's path.

"Get back, you big tub of lard!" Lizard warned murderously.

But Fat Stuff was taking no orders from Lizard. He didn't even slow down. Like a deadly reptile Lizard snapped into action. He aimed a lethal kick right at the center of Fat Stuff's midsection.

"Oof!"

Fat Stuff grunted pitifully as the cruel blow landed. He staggered back and his usually calm features were warped with pain turning into rage.

"You dirty fighter!" Fat Stuff cried.

The overweight native sprang like a tiger on Lizard. The two closed in, rolling over and over in the brush.

Now Jack faced The Claw alone. Keeping a cautious eye on the deadly blade on The Claw's wrist, he waited for the attack. It came with calculated deadliness, but he was ready. As the blade swished at him, the aviator ducked. Before The Claw could recover his balance, Jack caught the arm and grappled with the savage giant.

Jack would have preferred not having to pit his strength against this particular foe. The Claw was much the more powerful physically and had the added advantage of his weight. And Jack couldn't spar, using his naked fists against a knife. First he had to get the knife out of the way and then hope to land a knockout blow.

The Claw tripped Jack, but as Jack fell he pulled his opponent to the ground with him. The saw-like knife was raised to strike—Jack, with all his reserve strength, strained to hold back the blow. But the weight of the giant was too much: the deadly knife, razor sharp, moved closer and closer to Jack's throat.

In a desperate convulsive twist, Jack wriggled aside to escape the knife. But his head struck something immovable behind him. He could wriggle no farther—a heavy log blocked his movements.

Nearer and nearer to Jack's throat the saw-toothed knife descended. In a few short seconds it would sink home. In this crammed instant of eternity Jack's brain was racing at top speed. His body tensed, sending a final surge of strength against the upraised arm.

Then suddenly all the force restraining the giant arm was released. All that had barred The Claw from sinking his knife into Jack's body was pulled away. The knife descended with a rush, out of control.

But Jack's throat was not where the knife landed.

Instead, Jack had jerked his head aside just far enough —in spite of the log. He rolled out of the way of the descending blow with the wiriness of a trained wrestler. The knife struck the log behind Jack's head instead. It sank deeply into the wood and stuck.

Roaring with rage, The Claw jerked his arm to pull the blade out and it came loose from its socket.

The Claw stared dumbly at his disarmed member. Suddenly he realized that Jack was on his feet, ready now to use his fists in a more evenly matched battle.

"Now," Jack said, "for once in your life you've got to fight like a man—you yellow-livered gorilla."

The Claw was suddenly and almost pathetically afraid.

Shrinking back, he was on the point of running. Deprived of his weapon, he was as helpless as a babe. The sharp hook had been his badge of courage. Now, with only an empty socket on the leather-covered stump of his arm, he became craven and contemptible. The Claw shrank back from the flashing fists that already were beginning to land punishingly on his face and body.

Trying to cover, The Claw ducked his head. As he did so, Jack's fist swung upward and landed with crushing force on the monster's chin. The Claw groaned and sank to the ground, knocked completely out.

Jack glanced over his shoulder just in time to see Fat Stuff, who had been struggling with Lizard, land a telling blow on the back of Lizard's head. The punch ended that battle: Lizard dropped like a rock.

Fat Stuff looked with astonishment at his prostrate foe.

"Me no know me such a fighter!" the native exclaimed. "Someday me take boxin' lessons—self-defense!"

Jack grinned.

"Well, if you ask me—you don't need many lessons. That was a sweet K. O. you gave Lizard."

"Sweet for me. Sour for him." Fat Stuff chuckled. "The Claw look like him enjoy nice sleep, too. You good punch man also, Jack!"

"Well, let's get out of here before we have to do it all over again," Jack urged. "Where do we go from here?"

"Maybe find native village," Fat Stuff said, leading the way into the jungle once more.

They struck a path and the going became easier. The path led, Fat Stuff said, to the native village.

"Funny the natives stay on this island, with The Head likely to kidnap them for his prison," Jack said.

"Natives help Head catch escaped convicts!" Fat Stuff explained.

"What? And you're taking me to their village?"

"We go to village, but we take native boat without native see us," Fat Stuff elucidated happily.

Darkness fell, but they did not stop to rest. Night was the best time to commandeer one of the native boats.

The path grew wider and finally led into a moonlit clearing. Fat Stuff held up his hand. Ahead, scattered through the clearing, were a dozen native huts, perched on stilts to protect the occupants from tropical insects that crawled on the ground.

"Now we get real food!" Fat Stuff sighed. "An' a boat."

"We'd better be careful. Maybe someone's on guard." Fat Stuff shook his head.

"No guard, but native light sleeper. You stay here. Fat Stuff look for food."

The islander slipped away towards a near-by native hut. Soon he returned, bearing several parcels of food wrapped in green leaves.

"Sh-h!" he whispered. "Hold food—wait here. Me look for boat."

Again Fat Stuff drifted away into the shadows. Jack began to take stock of his surroundings. From the floor of a native hut not a dozen paces away hung a little cord. The cord would serve nicely to tie up the food packages so they could be carried more easily.

Creeping to the hut, Jack grasped the cord. He gave a quick jerk, trying to break it off.

Suddenly a scream rang out inside the dwelling.

The cord jerked itself out of his hand and disappeared through a crack in the floor.

It wasn't an ordinary cord! It was *human hair!*

"What you do, Jack?"

Fat Stuff had reappeared and was tugging at Jack's arm, trying to drag the aviator back into the jungle. But, as Jack turned, dark figures poured in a flood from other native huts.

"Oh-oh!" Fat Stuff groaned. "You makum much trouble now! Come—we gottum get 'way fast."

"No use, Fat Stuff!" Jack said, noting that the figures coming from the huts were natives armed with spears. "We're surrounded. What did I pull, the fire alarm?"

"You pull girl's hair," Fat Stuff explained. "Native custom. When girl wantum date with boy friend, her sleep with hair hanging through floor. Boy see hair. Him pull an' girl come out for date."

Jack had pulled the hair—but not gently. No wonder the response was a scream!

Guttural voices sounded threateningly on all sides. Suddenly a feminine voice called from the hut, and from the doorway emerged a native girl, clad in a sarong. She came down the ladder and looked at Jack. She turned to the natives, shook her head and spoke.

"She say you not her boy friend," Fat Stuff translated her words. "She say you stranger."

"Well, tell her I made a mistake. I don't want a date. I just want to go."

Fat Stuff spoke quickly to the girl, who shook her head once more.

"Her say she no let us go. She makum money by returnin' convict to prison."

"But they wouldn't do that to you!" Jack exclaimed. "You're a brother South Sea islander."

Fat Stuff wagged his head in denial.

"True an' not true," he said. "We same race, but not same tribe. We both in same boat, Jack. My tribe all time war their tribe. Fat Stuff no popular here."

Brown arms of native warriors seized Jack and Fat Stuff roughly. They were bound and trundled into an empty hut where they were left for the night.

In the morning the native girl brought them food.

"At least they treat us more humanely than The Head and Limehouse," Jack said.

Soon after their breakfast, Jack and Fat Stuff were marched along a path toward the other end of the island. The trail avoided the jungle, so they were able to make much more rapid time. By early afternoon they had reached the prison gate, which was opened by the smirking Limehouse.

"Well, well!" the guard exclaimed. "If it isn't Powder an' Fat Stuff! Welcome back to dear old Death Rock prison!"

Limehouse sent a guard with the natives to the administration building where they were to receive their reward. Then he escorted the two prisoners into the office of The Head.

The dwarfed spy blinked as he saw the American aviator again.

"You are always causing me trouble, Powder," The Head said. "I think it would be best if I killed you."

Jack did not answer. He stared straight at the little man, his jaw set firmly with determination not to weaken at any threat made by this international outlaw.

"But death would be too easy and it would rob me of a great deal of pleasure. I have other plans for you," The

Head went on in a pitiless monotone.

The Head was watching Jack closely, but if he expected any change in the American's expression, he was disappointed.

"Haven't you anything to say?"

For the first time since he was brought into the room, Jack spoke.

"My companion, Fat Stuff, should not be blamed for this escape," Jack said. "I engineered it and I persuaded him to accompany me."

"Is that true, Fat Stuff?" The Head asked.

"I not say," Fat Stuff replied.

"Virtually an admission," The Head said. "Well, since you were *forced* to go along with this renegade, I'm going to let you off with a short term in solitary."

The Head seemed to smile as he shifted his half closed eyes to Jack.

"But as for you, Powder—in view of your *very bad* prison record—I shall sentence you to five years in solitary confinement in Devil's Kitchen," he announced.

"*Oh!*"

The gasp came from feminine lips. Jack turned to see Betty Brown standing in the court room, her eyes aghast at the fate she had just heard meted out to "Powder Pellet."

CHAPTER FOURTEEN

DEVIL'S KITCHEN

Betty Brown, still pretty in spite of her drab prison dress and pale face, moved swiftly across the room and stood in front of The Head.

"Aren't you human at all?" she asked. "Five years in the Devil's Kitchen! Most convicts can't live even *five weeks* there!"

She glanced at Jack. Much was changed in him since she saw him soon after her arrival on the island. His hair had been shaved then, and he was dressed in a new convict's uniform. Those prison stripes now were soiled and dirty from his futile attempt to escape. His hair was growing out again—not blond as Powder Pellet's had been, but the dark hair of Smilin' Jack Martin.

As she noted the changes, Betty looked at Jack in puzzlement. Then she turned to The Head to repeat her plea.

"You *can't* send him there!"

"There is one way to keep Powder away from the Devil's Kitchen," The Head said, speaking in his usual sarcastic tone. "Once I offered him his freedom if he would help me get a bomber here, but he refused—"

"I still refuse," Jack cut in unhesitatingly.

"Perhaps a week or two in the Kitchen will change your mind," The Head said. "You are still unacquainted with that part of our prison where the cells are hewn from solid rock on a barren cliff. You can't escape from there, for the Kitchen is an island itself—separated from Death Rock by a narrow strait. Confinement in these rock ovens breaks a man quickly. A month will rob you of your mind—more than a month may kill you. Yes, maybe after you have tasted the ovens of the Kitchen, you will come round to my view."

"It's torture!" Betty said. "It's a punishment he doesn't deserve."

"I'm not so sure, Miss Brown," The Head said. "This man is a spy—he is not Powder, the man you once promised to marry."

Betty turned to Jack again, trying to place him in her mind.

"Where have I seen you before?" she asked. "You look familiar. I know it is not just your resemblance to Powder—"

Jack shook his head, trying vainly to halt the girl. But it was too late. A look of recognition sprang into her eyes.

"I know!" she cried. "In the fog near Memphis—at the airport in Valley Ridge. You are Smilin' Jack!"

"Ah!" The Head said, a note of satisfaction in his voice.

"And yet you doubt that he should be treated as a spy? Don't you know, Miss Brown, that it is an age-old custom in war for spies to pay with their lives when they are caught?"

Betty had been caught neatly in The Head's trap.

"You brought me here to make me give him away!" she said accusingly.

The Head smiled lazily and shook his head.

"No, Miss Brown," he told her calmly. "I was not aware that you and—ah—Smilin' Jack had met before, but your recognition makes the task simpler. I brought you here to urge you to dissuade him from sacrificing his mind and his life on the Kitchen. A word from you might persuade him to lure an American bomber here. Since you two know each other, perhaps it will be easier for you to convince him that—it would be best!"

Betty closed her lips tightly. It was easy to see that it was a struggle for her not to plead with Jack to save himself the torture of solitary confinement in the oven prison cells of Devil's Kitchen. But there was more at stake than one man's life—

"It is unnecessary for her to say anything," Jack said. "No matter what she said, I'd still refuse to help you—or any enemy of my country."

"Then it will be as you wish," The Head said, nodding to Limehouse. "You shall go to the Kitchen. And you, Miss Brown, will go there too, to comfort him. Oh—you needn't fear. You'll not be confined in a cell to lose your beauty and your mind. I have use for you later to force your father to let us employ the facilities of his airline to help our cause. But you will be near enough to see Smilin' Jack lose his smile, lose his mind—and lose his life. Then, perhaps, you will be more willing to persuade your father to help us."

The Head signaled Limehouse, who seized Jack's arm and turned him toward the door.

"Come along with me, Mr. 'Powder', or whatever your name is," he grunted. "The speedboat is ready to take you to the Kitchen."

A short time later a swift motor launch operated by a prison guard sped over the water toward a towering, precipitous rock standing off the coast of Death Rock Island. In the boat, guarded by Limehouse, were Smilin' Jack and Fat Stuff. Betty would be brought over later with a group of women to do the cooking and chores for prisoners in solitary confinement.

"The Head has made me special guard on the Kitchen," Limehouse said. "He ain't takin' no chances on your escapin' this time."

"Me hear no one ever escapum from there," Fat Stuff muttered.

"Yeah," Limehouse said, lighting a cigarette. "But there is always a first time, an' we don't care to let Smilin' Jack have that honor."

As the launch approached the isle, Jack saw a winding road running up from a wharf toward which the boat was making. Along this trail were small guardhouses, each watching over a tier of cells scooped out of the ledge of the perpendicular rock spire.

Escape was hardly possible under such close guard. Even if a man did manage to get out of his cell and past the guards, there remained the strait to swim in order to reach the main island. After that there was an ocean barring the way to freedom on the mainland.

"Thinkin' of swimmin' away from the Kitchen?" Limehouse grinned evilly as he watched Jack's eyes. "Let me remind you that even if a con did escape the Kitchen, he'd never reach the main island. The water here is lousy with sharks. They would rip a guy to ribbons in thirty seconds."

The boat came alongside the wharf, and Limehouse gruffly ordered his prisoners to disembark. As the boat swung around and headed back to Death Rock, Jack and Fat Stuff were ordered to march up the winding road.

The road was steep, and Jack already was exhausted from his exertions during the escape, but Limehouse allowed no rest.

From point to point the path branched off along ledges of the rock. Here were small steel cages, only a couple of feet above the ground and unprotected from the sun's glare, that marked the cells of solitary prisoners. The rest of each cell was solid rock, hewn four or five feet below the surface. With the hot sun beating down all day on the cells, it was easy to see how they became roasting ovens for the men inside.

Limehouse did not stop on the lower levels of cells. He sought to torture his prisoners by marching them up the path to the top tier, just below the flat summit of the rock.

Fat Stuff was ordered into one cell and Jack was placed in the next. It was dusk and too late for a meal, and the convicts were told that any clamor of protest would result in no breakfast.

A block of stone for a chair and a mattress on the rock floor were the only "furniture" in the cell. The small room, scarcely six feet by four, was hardly big enough for a man to turn around in—and it was unbearably hot, although the sun was sinking in the west.

Jack, exhausted from his ordeal, managed to drop off to sleep, but he was awakened at dawn by the arrival of guards with weak coffee and dried bread—breakfast.

Before Jack had finished the paltry meal, the heat of the day had set in. By noon the tropical sun was blazing through the iron grate above the ground. Jack was alone, with nothing to take his mind off his sufferings And his sentence was five years.

"Nothing to do—not a soul to talk to," Jack muttered to himself. "If a guy doesn't die from the heat here, he'll go nuts, all right, just from talking to himself."

Through the day Jack sat. Curious thoughts came to his mind. He likened himself to the hero of Jack London's "Sky Rover," the story of a convict who played at self-hypnotism in San Quentin. Jack tried to hypnotize himself, but in vain. However, there was one thing he could do—Jack recalled that in that story convicts communicated with other prisoners by tapping on the walls.

Jack sprang to his feet and removed one shoe. He tapped slowly on the wall of his cell. Fat Stuff was next door. He ought to hear the tapping.

No reply came.

Suddenly Jack realized why. Fat Stuff couldn't read or write—he couldn't spell messages ever if he wanted to!

Jack had no space in which to walk the floor of his cell. "A person never realizes what a bore he is until he's alone with himself continually," Jack decided.

Suddenly Jack tensed. Faintly, to his ears, came the sound of music:

"Da-da—*de-dee-dah!* Ump-pum-de-dee-dah!"

Was Jack losing his mind? Was he hearing things?

The voice came nearer.

"Betty!" Jack gasped, pushing his face close to the bars.

"Sh-h!" the girl whispered. "I'm bringing you your lunch, but I can't talk to you."

Through a small opening in the cage, Betty pushed some food—a kind of porridge—and water.

"You're an angel!" Jack said. "Even seeing you at meal time is going to make my stay in this cell a lot easier to take!"

"O-o-o h—if I had th' wings of an angel," Betty sang, "over these prison walls I would fly-y-y—"

Smiling, Betty moved on about her task of feeding the prisoners. Jack, however, did not eat the food. Instead, he was thinking of the words to the song. They ran through his mind again and again.

"Fly! With wings! That's the answer!" Jack whispered hoarsely to himself. "I'm no sailor—I'm a pilot. I won't go by sea, but by air. I'll fly—some way. I'll get wings!"

Seating himself on his pallet he ate slowly, absorbed

Jack Caught a Glimpse of a Plane on Dawn Patrol

in thought. By degrees a plan formed in his mind—a desperate plan, one that depended on sheer daring for success. But Jack's position was desperate and only a desperate plan could succeed. One day of suffering in the Kitchen proved that he could not last long here. If his mission for Uncle Sam was not to fail, he had to escape *now!*

Through the hours of darkness Jack tossed on his hard bed. He didn't know how he'd escape, but he would. Once away from this island, he could terminate the careers of The Head and his gang. He could obtain the release of men unjustly held in confinement. An American destroyer or a few bombers could take the island and blast its torture chambers to bits.

Dawn was breaking while Jack still studied his problem. Then faintly from the northwest came the sound of airplane motors. Jack caught a glimpse of the craft—a U. S. Navy bomber on dawn patrol.

A wild idea flashed into his mind. Wings of an airplane did not always need a motor.

"A glider! That's it! If I can get out of this cell I might be able to build a glider. I could launch it when one of those patrol bombers flew over. I could attract the crew's attention, land on the water and they'd pick me up."

Footsteps interrupted Jack's train of thought. Someone was coming.

"Hello, Powder!" came a raspy greeting.

Limehouse stood outside the cell.

"I hope that bomber didn't make you homesick."

Jack stood at the bars of his prison, looking up at Limehouse.

"A lot of difference it would make to you if it did!" Jack replied. "Say, how often do the bombers fly over?"

"What do you care?" Limehouse taunted. "You're not goin' out to meet one. But those bombers won't bother you much longer."

"What do you mean?"

"Death Rock ain't United States territory an' The Head has sent word to the gov'ment official in his pay in South America protestin' against the bomber flyin' over this island. He'll get the American ambassador to change the patrol route—prob'ly in a week or so."

Limehouse laughed tauntingly. The prison guard delighted in tormenting his prisoners. He wanted Jack to know that even the sight of friendly airplanes was to be taken away.

Jack tried to keep his face from showing his anxiety. The news meant that if he were to escape he had to do it within a week's short time.

Limehouse continued to torment Jack and the other prisoners in the tier of cells. Pulling a package of cigarettes from his pocket, Limehouse thrust one into his mouth, knowing how the men in the cells longed for a forbidden smoke.

Taking a small lighter from his pocket, Limehouse deliberately snapped it to light the cigarette. But the lighter failed to work. Jack concealed a smile. Limehouse tried again to make the lighter work—again it failed, and again he tried.

The prison guard's temper mounted as he felt himself humiliated by his own cigarette lighter. With an exclamation of disgust, Limehouse flung the lighter to the rocky ledge, turned on his heel and strode away.

Jack let his mind revert to his own problem. This problem was much more pressing than a cigarette lighter that failed to work. Jack was studying how the heat, reflected from this rocky mountain spire, would warm the air, thus producing a thermal updraft which could easily lift a small glider high into the air.

But Jack didn't have a glider and his cell was obviously much too small in which to build one. Jack's foremost problem was to get out of his cell to build such a glider. If he could only make a rude key, but he had no metal.

No metal?

An object glinted on the rock ledge in front of Jack's cell—the discarded cigarette lighter! Metal, if Jack could only reach it, fully eight feet away! Jack's arm stretched through the bars, hopelessly.

A pole or something! But there was nothing in the cell to extend Jack's reach. The metal tantalized Jack, glistening there in the early morning sunlight.

Then a thought struck him. He removed his jacket. Holding onto one sleeve he tossed it at the lighter, trying to sweep it toward the cell. But the jacket was too short.

"My pants!"

Removing his striped trousers, Jack tied them to the sleeve of the jacket. Again he tried to toss them over the lighter. Everything depended on accuracy. His first aim was bad. His second touched the lighter, but failed to budge it. The job would require skill and dogged persistence. Again and again he tried.

At last, success! A loose thread on the trousers caught the lid of the broken lighter. Slowly Jack pulled it toward him, bringing it within arm's reach.

He seized it hastily and drew it into the cell.

"I've got it!" he cried in a hoarse whisper of triumph.

Peering out through the bars, Jack made sure his actions had gone undetected by the watchmen in the guardhouse at the end of the ledge. But no one was abroad at this time of the day. The heat was growing intense and guards preferred the cooler shade.

Jack put on his trousers and set to work. Knocking the lighter apart, he used his stone seat to straighten out the metal. Then he began working the edges of the flattened tube against the rock.

For hours he sat, grinding the metal against the jagged edges of the stone seat. Slowly and painstakingly he was transforming the bit of metal into the semblance of a key.

This key would open the way to freedom!

There was enough silicon in the rock to give it an emery surface. The task would be tedious and painstaking, but eventually the job would be finished and Smilin' Jack would have a skeleton key with which to unlock his cell.

As the afternoon wore on and the heat grew less intense, guards paid their regulation visits to the cell. Jack hid his handicraft. The soiled bed was removed, the prisoners were taken out for exercise, and Jack was given a change of clothing.

Every time the guards unlocked Jack's cell, the aviator studied the contour of the key, fixing it in mind so that he could adapt his bit of metal to the general form.

Betty arrived with the evening meal just before sundown.

"I'm going to try to escape," Jack whispered to the girl.

"Jack! They'll kill you!" Betty spoke in a low voice that could not be overheard by the guards who were watching her serve the meal to the prisoners.

"No they won't, and if I don't escape I'll die!" Jack said. "I need clothing—not men's clothing but silk clothing."

"Are you going to dress like a woman, Jack?" Betty asked. "You might masquerade as Powder, but not as a girl. You're too big—"

"Never mind what I need clothing for," Jack said. "Where can I get silk dresses—"

"Limehouse has a daughter," Betty whispered. "She lives in his house—up on top of the mountain."

"Get a move on!" one of the guards shouted at Betty. Betty quickly rose and moved away.

After dinner, the prisoners were left alone by the guards. Jack used this opportunity to file on his key, duplicating as closely as possible the original he had seen used by the guards.

Through the night he scraped, keeping his ears alert for sound of the guard's footsteps.

When dawn arrived, Jack had a crude key.

"Locks have been picked with much simpler objects," Jack said. "If this doesn't work I'm stuck here for the rest of my life."

Gingerly Smilin' Jack reached his arm through the bars of his cell.

"If it does work I'm still stuck—stuck with the problem of how to build a glider out of thin air!" he added.

The key slipped into the lock. The crucial moment had come!

CHAPTER FIFTEEN

A WEIRD CONTRAPTION

The makeshift key fitted but it would not turn. Jack withdrew it from the lock and filed some more. Trying again, he turned the key with difficulty. There was a sharp click and the door was open.

"It works!" Jack gloated in a throaty whisper.

He closed the door, but it would not relock. Again it was necessary to file and again he was successful. Now the key was perfect. It would lock and unlock the door. But it was daylight now. Soon the guards would be stirring and the construction of the glider would have to wait until after dark that night.

But from what could he fabricate any sort of glider at all?

Hiding his key under the rock seat in his cell, Jack went through the day's routine. Having made some headway, Jack found the heat not so unbearable now, nor did Limehouse's visit rankle him so much. Jack would be free before long—he hoped!

That night, Jack thought quiet would never descend on the tiers of cells. A prisoner on the level below was screaming and guards were trying to quiet him. But at last there was silence and Jack removed his key from its hiding place.

The door opened again without difficulty. What now? The trail down the side of the rock spire was so heavily guarded Jack could not expect to reach the base without discovery. He had to find the materials for his glider somewhere up above.

Slipping along the cells, past sleeping prisoners, Jack followed the trail. He avoided guardhouses by creeping behind and around them. The guards were dozing, believing that all prisoners were securely locked in their cells. Even if one did escape his cell, there wasn't a chance for him to reach safety across the shark-infested strait between the Devil's Kitchen and Death Rock.

At last Jack reached the top of the rock. A shadowy, barred structure loomed ahead of him in the light of the new moon. At first Jack thought he had run across a special cell of some sort. Then, as he crept closer he saw that the bars were not of steel, but of bamboo.

The "cell" was an old bamboo arbor constructed on top of the rock, possibly in a futile attempt to grow grapes or other vines.

Jack's heart beat rapidly. That bamboo would be just the thing for making longerons and wing spars for a glider!

"Why, I'm as good as sprouting wings right now!" Jack exclaimed to himself triumphantly.

But the problem was not so easily solved. There was wing fabric to consider. Jack already had an idea of what he could use for wing fabric. Betty had told him that Limehouse had a daughter. Girls mean clothes—clothes for a young woman ought to include lots of silk.

Silk would be the solution to Smilin' Jack's wing-fabric problem.

Following the path down from the top, Jack made his way toward the row of cottages which housed members of the families of the guards. The large, two-story house at the end undoubtedly was Limehouse's, for he was in charge of the guards on Devil's Kitchen.

The house was dark. Everyone was sleeping. Jack crept cautiously toward it, knowing that if he should arouse anyone in the house, he would be cruelly punished. Limehouse was not the kind of a man to miss an opportunity to punish with a vengeance.

A figure moved in the shadows. Jack tensed. Someone was coming.

Into the moonlight came a tiny creature. Not a man, but a small monkey—undoubtedly a pet of Limehouse's daughter.

"Scram!" Jack whispered.

The monkey disappeared into the house through an open window.

Smiling, the American aviator followed the monkey. Under cover of darkness he made his way into the house. Upstairs a door was ajar, and Jack peeked through the door. Limehouse was snoring in a bed in that room.

Restraining his desire to repay Limehouse for some of the things he had done, Jack tried the room across the hall. The scent of perfume told Jack that this was the place he sought. The room was occupied by Limehouse's daughter.

Moonlight streaming through the window revealed the door of the clothes closet. Jack pulled it open and stepped inside.

"Boy!" he thought as he ran his hands over the garments.

Limehouse's daughter had more clothing than a Fifth Avenue gown shop!

Jack grinned to himself as he filled his arms with silken dresses. Limehouse would certainly boil if he knew he had unwittingly provided for Smilin' Jack's escape.

Jack, with an armload of clothing, turned to go when suddenly a hand fell on his shoulder!

He was caught! This was the end.

Jack waited. A tender little finger stroked his ear.

It was the monkey Jack had met outside the house. The animal had followed him to the girl's room.

Jack sighed in relief, but to his dismay a coat hanger fell from the rack and clattered to the floor.

The girl's gentle breathing ceased.

"Who's there?" came a timid voice from the bed.

Jack's heart almost stopped. The girl had awakened.

"Who's there?" the girl repeated. "I know I heard someone!"

Jack heard the movement of the girl in the bed. If she turned on the light, escape would be impossible.

Jack's only hope was to answer the question in a way that would relieve the girl's fears. How? A sudden idea came to his mind.

Laying aside the clothing, Jack reached down and stroked the monkey, which had jumped to the floor at the sound of the girl's voice. His fingers tickled the creature's ribs. A startled squeal came from the monkey.

The simian, like human beings, was ticklish.

Squealing, the monkey ran across the room and hopped on the girl's bed. A sigh of relief came from her as her fears subsided.

"Oh!" she exclaimed. "So it was only you, Ringtail. What a bad little monkey you were to frighten me so! Now be quiet so I can go back to my dreams."

As the girl talked sleepily to Ringtail, Smilin' Jack slipped quietly out of the house. He made his way past Limehouse's door to the downstairs rooms. There he managed to find a sewing basket and a kitchen knife. But the thread in the sewing basket, while it would serve some purposes, was not strong enough for others. He needed wire or heavy cord at least. There seemed to be none in the house.

Leaving the place, Jack strolled through the shadows to the end of the row of cottages occupied by guards. At the far end was a little shed, from which came a buzzing.

"The electric dynamo!" Jack exclaimed. "There ought to be wire there!"

There was, in large quantities. Jack took as much as he thought he would need and then hurried away. A light-sleeping guard might interrupt Jack's plan and he did not care to take the risk of being seen by delaying within view of the guards' homes.

He found the top of the rock deserted as before. He set to work, laboring by the light of the stars. First he notched the bamboo ribs taken from the arbor. Using the kitchen knife he cut them into proper lengths.

The ribs were tied with wire to the main spar and the outline of the glider began to take shape.

Then, in the midst of his work, Jack heard a noise behind him. Turning quickly, Jack saw a shadow on the ground. But Jack was not upset this time. He recognized the shadow.

It was Ringtail, the monkey, come to pay another visit.

"Stick around, little fellow," Jack greeted the monkey. "Any kind of companionship does a fellow good in this forsaken place."

Through the night Jack worked, and when the first tint of dawn appeared on the eastern horizon, he hastily hid his tools and materials in a crevice and rushed down the trail to his cell. He reached the cell just as dawn was breaking, but he got there ahead of the guards making their morning rounds.

Jack hoped that the whittlings from his bamboo poles would not be found during the day and arouse suspicion.

"All I can do is to pray that no one blunders up on the mountain top," Jack said to himself as he slipped the key in the lock of his cell and closed it for the day.

He hid the key under the rock seat in his cell. As long as he had that key he had hope.

Jack went through the routine of the daylight hours, sweltering in the heat of his oven-cell, occasionally snatching bits of sleep as he waited for night to come.

Limehouse missed his usual round that day, and this struck Jack as ominous.

Late in the afternoon Betty appeared with the rations. She stooped beside Jack's cell.

"Jack!" she whispered. "What have you done?"

For a moment Jack's heart sank. Had his plan to escape been discovered?

"Done?"

"Someone has taken all the silk dresses Limehouse's daughter had!" Betty exclaimed. "There's a terrible commotion in the cottages."

"But what have I to do with it?" Jack asked, not daring to tell Betty the truth for fear of being overheard.

"You asked me about silk dresses day before yesterday," Betty said.

Smilin' Jack grinned and Betty winked.

"Tell me about it, Betty," he pleaded.

Betty glanced over her shoulder. The guards were busy abusing a prisoner and they weren't noticing her.

"When Laura—that's Limehouse's daughter—woke up yesterday morning she noticed some of her dresses missing," Betty related. "She told Limehouse, who blamed the convicts and threatened to search every prisoner here from head to foot.

"When Mrs. Limehouse heard of the theft of her daughter's dresses, she laid out her husband for letting someone steal the clothes from under his nose. Limehouse ordered a search of the women prisoners—that's how I happened to hear the story. But of course nothing was found.

"No one seemed to consider that a man might have taken the clothes—besides, the male prisoners here are all in solitary—locked tight in their cells. The only other solution was that women were stealing from each other. Mrs. Limehouse accused the daughter of another guard. Laura accused the wife of the pier guard. The wives have been fighting all day. The whole place is in an uproar. How on earth did you do it, Jack, and what are you up to?"

Jack was chuckling softly at the news, even though he realized that it would lead to worse punishment than ever if he were caught.

"I haven't time to tell you now, Betty," he said to the girl. "But I will some day, if everything works out. You'd better be moving along now, before the guards notice how long you've been talking to me."

"They won't notice," Betty laughed. "They've got troubles of their own. But—I—I hope your plan works, Jack! And *do* be careful!"

With those words, Betty moved away from the cell. Jack watched her go, hoping that, before long now, he would escape and bring rescuers here to release her and Fat Stuff.

The theft of Laura's clothing caused such a stir on Devil's Kitchen that the guards were too occupied to abuse the prisoners that day. In fact, the cells were scarcely visited and Jack managed to get in considerable sleep.

Had time not been so pressing, Jack would have enjoyed doing a little further sabotage of the prison guards' morale, but he had to escape before the route of the patrol plane was changed.

Jack heard the plane come over every morning, but it might shift its course at any time.

As soon as the cells were quiet when night came again, Jack removed his rudely fashioned key from its hiding place and opened his barred door.

Hurrying to the mountain top, he again set to work on his glider. The rude materials and tools were difficult to handle, but Jack's experience as an aviator overcame the handicaps. Besides, he *had* to work fast. The time left for him to succeed in making good his escape grew less each day that passed.

There were other possibilities, besides lack of time, that haunted him.

"Even to hope that this chicken coop will fly is a strain on a fellow's imagination," Jack muttered as he worked with the kitchen knife.

The moon, which had been shining brightly, was dimming beneath clouds that suddenly covered the sky. Soon after midnight it began to rain.

Ordinarily Jack would have welcomed rain as bringing relief from the suffocating heat. But now the rain meant delay in the completion of his glider.

He pulled his framework to the crevice and lowered it out of sight, hanging its tail on a projecting rock. The crevice furnished a safe hiding place unless a thorough search were made. But Jack had to pray that there would be no thorough search. There was no other hiding place available.

Jack ran back toward his cell as the rain fell, drenching him to the skin. He fervently hoped no rain would fall the next night, because, if it did, he might never get his glider completed before the patrol plane ceased flying near Death Rock.

The rain ceased as Jack locked himself in his cell. He was damp, but comfortably relieved from the heat.

Gazing from the barred doorway he saw he had a visitor. Ringtail, the monkey, was squatting outside. With a squeak of joy, Ringtail sprang through the bars, landing on Smilin' Jack, splattering mud over his prison uniform.

"You little pest!" Jack exclaimed, seizing Ringtail and thrusting him back outside the cell again. "If the guards see that mud on me, they'll get wise that I've been sneakin' out."

Jack managed to scrape off the mud with his hands, but as he did so he noticed that there was mud on his shoes also.

"Good night!" Jack exclaimed as a new thought dawned on him. "That means tracks!"

Suddenly Jack realized that he had left a trail from his cell to the top of the mountain and that this trail led directly to the spot where he had hidden his makeshift glider.

In a flash Jack was out of his cell. Once more he climbed past the guardhouse and up the trail to the top of the

mountain. He cut a small length of bamboo from the
arbor and, using it as a trowel to cover his tracks he
started down, and erased each track as he went back to
the cell.

It was a laborious job and a long one. He barely finished before the rising of the sun. The building of his
glider was more than a simple construction job!

Before the guard appeared for the morning check-up,
Jack heard the patrol bomber pass overhead again. Tomorrow morning he hoped to be in the air to meet it:
a strange flier in a stranger aerial contraption!

"And I'll be there—if everything works out!" he
vowed, lying down on his lumpy mattress.

The excitement caused by the theft of the girl's dresses
still had not died down on this second day. Again the
convicts were spared the usual harsh treatment as the
guards quarreled and bickered among themselves.

Jack saw Betty again, but she was being watched by her
guard and there was no time to exchange more than a
greeting. Jack had hoped to be able to tell her that he
planned to escape that night. But he didn't dare risk it.

When Jack left his cell that night, however, he did not
go directly up the trail. Instead, he crept to the cell next
to his and tossed a pebble inside.

"Fat Stuff!" he whispered.

A grunt came from within the cell. A moment later
Fat Stuff's round face peered through the bars.

"Jack!" Fat Stuff's sleepy eyes opened wide as he saw
his visitor. "What you do? How you gettum out your

cell?"

"Sh-h!" Jack whispered, fearful lest other prisoners learn he was outside his cell. "I haven't time to tell you now, Fat Stuff, but I'm going to try to make a break for it tonight. Maybe I'll be back for you later."

"You not takum me?" Fat Stuff asked with disappointment in his voice.

Jack shook his head.

"Can't," he said "It hurts to think I have to leave you, but it's impossible to take you now. So I came to say good-by—wish me luck, and I'll return for you, old-timer."

Tears dripped from Fat Stuff's eyes. His chubby hand came through the bars to clasp Jack's.

"Good luck an' good-by, Jack." he said quietly.

"Don't give up hope, Fat Stuff." Jack told his friend as he shook the chubby hand. "If I get away it won't be good-by for long. I've a scheme that may set you free."

With those parting words, Jack slipped off into the darkness and made his way past the guardhouses to the summit of the rocky mountain. He took his framework from its hiding place. With needle and thread he set to work stretching the silken dresses taut over the wings and tail.

When Smilin' Jack thought of the beautiful gliders he had seen at Elmira and then looked at his creation, he groaned aloud.

"It sure gives me a sort of pancake-landing feeling in the pit of my stomach," he said to himself. "But this is the best I could do with a girl's dresses, wire and bamboo. I wish this glider were strong enough to take Fat Stuff along, too, but it'll be a miracle if it even carries me."

Jack stitched the final silk piece in place and stood back to survey the product of his labor. It was finished. The first streaks of dawn were appearing in the east and it would soon be time for the dawn patrol.

Everything depended on the trial flight. If it failed, there could be no more.

CHAPTER SIXTEEN

WAITING FOR THE DAWN

Realizing that daylight would come in a very few moments, Jack tried to dismiss a feeling of uneasiness as he waited for the distant drone of airplane motors which would herald the approach of the patrol bomber.

What if The Head's protest to the government of the United States, through the bribed official, already had resulted in altering the course of bombers passing near Death Rock? If the patrol failed to arrive, guards quickly would discover Smilin' Jack missing as they made their early morning check-up of the prisoners. After that Jack would surely be apprehended, for the guards would comb every inch of the Rock.

The first flaming segment of the sun appeared over the horizon in the east. Too late to turn back now, Jack thought, for he couldn't possibly reach his cell without being observed by the awakened guards.

Where was that patrol bomber? Why on earth didn't it show up? It was late!

Jack made a few final adjustments after an inspection of his makeshift glider. Then he pulled it close to the edge of the precipitous mountain. Alongside the glider ran the crevice which had afforded him a hiding place for the machine. There would be no time to hide it now, if the guards discovered Jack was missing. He might hide there himself, but the crevice was deep and filled with jagged rocks. A slip of his foot and he might crash a hundred feet to his death in some cavern below.

Jack stood beside his improvised flying machine, ready to take off the moment the Navy plane appeared.

Already the heat of the tropical sun was beginning to make itself felt, but Jack welcomed the heat today. It meant that currents of air were rising from Devil's Kitchen and these currents would help lift the glider into the air.

This high rock was ideal for glider flying.

But Jack's worry was not about flying. It was about the tardy bomber. He sat down and waited. He stood up and waited. He walked in circles and waited. He simply waited. But still no patrol bomber appeared.

The sun now was up. Guards already were beginning their rounds of the Kitchen's torture cells. In a few minutes Jack's escape would be known and Limehouse, enraged to the exploding point, would run the gamut of punishments when Jack was caught. Nothing would be too severe to inflict on this prisoner who had escaped a second time. Jack resolved not to be caught if he could help it—he'd take off in his glider anyway and try to remain aloft until the Navy craft appeared. Even a crash into the sea was better than recapture.

There was still no sign of the awaited plane.

Jack crept to the rim of the summit of the rock to look down on the activities of the guards below. They

Jack Waited Impatiently for the Plane

were making their morning check-up now, visiting cells, rousing prisoners with the customary harsh treatment.

Limehouse was there, awakening the men in Jack's own tier of cells. From Limehouse's actions, Jack judged that the chief guard was still ill-tempered because he had found no clues concerning the disappearance of Daughter Laura's dresses. If Jack were caught, that mystery would be explained and Limehouse would have his culprit.

Limehouse was working along the cells from the opposite end from which Jack's was located. Jack's empty cell would be the last to be visited. This was a break, but Jack was afraid it would not be enough. Even though Limehouse delayed visiting the cells in the tier for several minutes, that time would be needed for Jack to get into the air once he saw the patrol bomber.

Ten minutes before his escape was discovered was about the most Jack could expect.

Limehouse was in his bitterest mood. At one cell he flew into a rage, probably because of some imagined "insolence" on the part of a half-crazed prisoner. The chief of guards reached inside the cell and struck the helpless man.

From cell to cell Limehouse continued his abusive activity. At last he reached Fat Stuff's rock chamber, the second from the last one and the cell next to Jack's.

Limehouse called for the prisoner to appear. Apparently there was no answer, for Limehouse knelt and peered inside. Fat Stuff was unusually slow to awaken this morning. Limehouse picked up a rock and threw it into the cell. Still the chubby native failed to arouse himself. Limehouse threw another missile.

"Good old Fat Stuff!" Smilin' Jack muttered as he watched the scene on the ledge below. "He's trying to give me extra time by delaying Limehouse. As long as Limehouse keeps trying to awaken Fat Stuff and as long as Fat Stuff keeps stalling, I've got a chance!"

Limehouse was growing angrier and angrier as Fat Stuff apparently refused to wake up. The guard impatiently rattled the bars of the cell. Thus failing to arouse the sleeping islander, Limehouse took his keys from his pocket and unlocked the door. Limehouse shouted loud ly for Fat Stuff to get up.

"Rise an' shine or I'll beat you to a pulp!" Limehouse yelled at the top of his lungs.

But even this threat seemed not to have a great deal of effect on Fat Stuff, who apparently had decided it would take more than shouts to get him up this morning.

Limehouse climbed into the cell. A moment later he reappeared, dragging Fat Stuff out after him.

Limehouse was scolding, raging, pouring abuse on the unfortunate islander. But Fat Stuff was taking it all, standing there stolidly, letting Limehouse rave. Limehouse raised his fist and pounded it into Fat Stuff's face.

Jack's blood boiled as he witnessed the bullying actions of the guard. Some day Limehouse would pay dearly for those cowardly blows.

But Fat Stuff now had stalled as long as he could. There was a limit to even Limehouse's ability to hand out cruelties. Tired of punishing Fat Stuff, he shoved the chubby islander back into his cell. The door was closed and locked behind him.

"Now I'm in for it," Jack said as Limehouse turned to visit the cell from which Jack had escaped.

Once more Smilin' Jack glanced into the sky, hoping for a sign of the Navy patrol bomber winging toward the island, but the sky still was clear. There was not even the buzz of an insect to be heard and mistaken for the roar of a plane's motors.

Limehouse strode to Jack's cell. Stopping in front of the cell, Limehouse shouted for Jack. There was no answer. For the second time the guard lost his temper. He knelt by the bars and shouted. Still no answer. Without realizing that the cell was empty the guard tossed a handful of rock through the bars, at the same time calling a third demand for "Powder" to "rise an' shine."

There was still no answer. None could come from an empty cell.

Limehouse strained his eyes peering into the semi-darkness of the cell. Even from the top of the mountain, Jack could see incredulity course through the body of the angry guard as he saw nothing in the cell. Limehouse always had regarded his solitary confinement cells as escape-proof.

As Limehouse stared, the incredulity was replaced by

the realization that one prisoner, at least, had found a way out. Limehouse sprang to his feet.

Jack's escape had been discovered and the patrol bomber still had not appeared.

Limehouse cupped his hands in front of his mouth. His voice, shrill with excitement and rage, echoed from the rock prison:

"Guards! Guards!"

Two men ran from their station in the near-by guardhouse. As they reached Limehouse, he pointed and gesticulated wildly at Jack's empty cell. The guards apparently could not believe him, for they knelt and looked inside, then rose shaking their heads, unbelievingly.

It was impossible for a man to escape from a cell in the Devil's Kitchen!

One of the guards kicked the door. To the further amazement of the three men, the door swung open.

The rage of Limehouse and his men magnified itself a thousand times. Limehouse stamped his feet on the ground. Where did "Powder" get a key? His voice roared in rage so that it could be heard to the top of the mountain:

"Sound the general alarm! He's got to be somewhere on this island. He couldn't possibly get away! Rout out all the guards! We'll find that culprit, or I'll break every guard on duty!"

The two guards sprang into instant action. They raced back to the guardhouse. A moment later the wail of a siren gave the alarm, notifying all guards on the Kitchen that a prisoner had escaped.

Jack's position on top of the mountain was perilous. He might easily be spotted as he watched the activities below. He left his post and hurried back to his glider, ready to take off. Vainly he searched the sky for the thousandth time. But no patrol bomber flew this course today.

The guards were searching every nook and cranny now for a trace of the escaped prisoner. Probably some of them already were on their way to the summit.

The hot sun was climbing in the sky and warm currents of air were tugging at the silken fabrics of Smilin' Jack's home-made glider.

For a few moments Jack was tempted to risk a takeoff. Gliders might be kept aloft indefinitely in suitable air currents, but not Jack's makeshift affair. He would be lucky if it flew at all, but he had hopes born of desperation. In Jack's case it was all or nothing. If he took off too soon, those planes secretly based on Death Rock might shoot him down while he soared waiting for the bomber. Or, if the glider failed to stay aloft, sharks in the ocean would tear him to pieces when he came down in the sea.

On the other hand, to remain on the rock meant certain capture. All of Jack's studied plans would come to naught.

Was it worth the risk? Should he take off?

The decision was taken out of Jack's hands at that moment. A sharp cry came from the path up the cliff.

Wheeling, Jack saw Limehouse topping the summit.

The guard saw the glider and gaped at the sight of the multicolored silks stretched over a framework of bamboo. He trained an automatic pistol at Jack and roared:

"So you're the dirty thief who stole my daughter's clothes! You'll get the guillotine for this!"

Limehouse stumbled up the last few steps of the path. Jack was tempted to spring into the glider and take off, but such a move could only be fatal. Before Jack could leap, Limehouse would riddle him with bullets.

Limehouse's first flush of anger subsided. Realizing the prisoner was at his mercy, the guard decided to get a little personal revenge before returning Jack to his cell.

Approaching slowly, keeping the pistol pointed at Jack, Limehouse appraised the workmanship of the glider. A nasty little smile crept over his face.

"Well, well!" he spoke. "An aviation expert! Wonderful guy, ain't you?"

Chuckling at his sarcasm, Limehouse moved toward Jack. His expression was taunting, his eyes were narrow slits, hiding cruel, jeering gleams.

"I don't suppose you had any idea of usin' this little flyin' machine in an attempt to make connection with the American dawn patrol today, did you?" the guard asked.

Smilin' Jack saw no reason to reply. His eyes watched every move Limehouse made, seeking a chance to turn the tables. If Limehouse would only shift the muzzle of the gun for a brief instant!

But Limehouse was cautious. Even when he stopped

to pick up a length of bamboo for a club, the aim did not waver. Hefting the club, Limehouse still kept the gun trained. He advanced toward the glider, raising his cudgel, ready to land a wing-shattering blow.

"My heart bleeds to think of havin' to destroy such a work of art," he said sarcastically. "But our little institution is rather old-fashioned. We frown upon convicts becomin' air minded."

The club was poised for a blow, but as Limehouse spoke he forgot for a second to keep the pistol aimed. This was the chance Jack waited for! He dived at the prison guard, desperation propelling him with such speed that he was upon the surprised prison official before Limehouse could fire.

Limehouse squeezed the trigger, but the bullets whistled wildly wide of their mark as Jack drove his fists into the guard's body with punishing force. Limehouse rocked back on his heels. He dropped the club as he strove to maintain his balance. Jack caught the wrist of the gun hand, giving it a wrench.

Howling with pain, Limehouse's fingers released their grip on the pistol. The automatic clattered to the rocks, bouncing and sliding and finally crashing into the deep crevice where Smilin' Jack had hidden the glider during its secret construction.

Jack's sudden attack threw Limehouse on the defensive. The guard quickly regained his footing and directed a blow which landed harmlessly on Jack's shoulder. The two men grappled. Limehouse brought up his knee, seeking to plant it in the pit of Jack's stomach with crippling force. Again Jack was wary. He had expected such tactics from Limehouse. Swinging his fist, Smilin' Jack managed to land a prodigious blow which checked the attempt to disable him.

Limehouse roared and attacked with redoubled fury. He butted and kicked, but Smilin' Jack skillfully dodged. Another blow with Jack's free hand sent Limehouse sprawling. Jack dived on top of his foe, mauling the prison guard with his fists, trying to land a knockout punch.

But Limehouse was tough. He was hard to put out of action. Locked in a desperate struggle, the two men rolled over and over on the ground, approaching closer and closer to the edge of the crevice.

Below the fighting men came cries of other guards, rushing up the trail at the sound of the pistol shots. Jack had to finish his antagonist before reinforcements arrived.

Jack was tiring rapidly. His long confinement, his lack of good food and the grueling heat of the solitary cells had robbed the aviator of his stamina. Limehouse, on the other hand, had been hardened by his daily duties. Limehouse fought confidently, fully aware that Jack's imprisonment had sapped his endurance.

But there was a factor that Limehouse overlooked: Jack's mind was keener and quicker than the guard's. Jack's brain had been trained as an aviator to act in split seconds.

The two men hung on the rim of the crevice. Limehouse tried to push Jack over the brink, but Jack slipped away and sprang to his feet. Limehouse came after him—again the two men locked arms. Limehouse pushed Jack backward toward the glider, hoping that Jack would fall and smash the machine, and perhaps injure himself in the wreckage.

But for a slight second Limehouse left himself open. Jack landed a blow that toppled them the other way. They landed at the brink of the yawning crack in the rock. Jack's foot slipped over the edge and hung down in the death-trap of a hole. Summoning all his energy, Limehouse tried to shove Jack the rest of the way, but desperation sent a flood of new energy into Jack. Pushing the guard back, Jack landed a powerful left which knocked the warden momentarily aside. When Limehouse closed in again, Jack was on his feet, crouching like a professional boxer moving in for a knockout.

Disregarding additional punishment from Smilin' Jack's fists, Limehouse charged with his head down, butting Jack backward toward the rim of the pit. With the quickness of a cat, Jack caught himself and counter-attacked.

Deadlocked, the two men stood toe to toe, sparring at the edge of the deep ravine. Jabbing and ducking, Jack wove in and out, parrying blows and sparring. This tricky sort of fighting was not Limehouse's style. He saw that Jack would be an easy victor if something wasn't done quickly. Jack's steady rain of blows had landed a neat score of bruises. One of the guard's eyes was closed; his face was swollen and bloody.

Slowly Limehouse retreated from the edge of the precipice. His good eye gleamed with a new cunning. Suddenly his hand flashed inside his coat and whipped out a long, sharp knife.

Limehouse's mouth opened with a nasty grin. He chuckled with evil anticipation as he closed in toward Jack, ready to use the knife on his opponent.

Jack realized the desperate nature of his situation. He was tired, panting and at the verge of exhaustion, and his foe had a weapon far more effective than Jack's bare fists.

Jack slowly retreated as Limehouse advanced. Back, nearer and nearer to the ravine, the two men moved. Limehouse held the knife ready to plunge it into Jack.

Suddenly Limehouse sprang, the weapon upraised. Jack was at the edge of the ravine, unable to retreat farther.

Even as the guard sprang, Jack's alert senses caught the sound of something he had been waiting for—the four-motored drone of a seaplane. The patrol bomber was coming, but Jack, locked in this desperate battle, could not get to the glider.

Realizing there was only one way out of the trap, Smilin' Jack whirled and sprang.

His body flashed across the abyss, barely reaching the other side. Catching his balance, Jack turned and faced Limehouse, who was ready to jump.

CHAPTER SEVENTEEN

THE FLYING WARDROBE

Limehouse, eyes glittering as he anticipated the finish of his opponent, launched himself across the chasm. He landed on the other side and braced himself for Jack's rushing attack.

The knife slashed viciously at Jack's chest, but the aviator quickly twisted his body so that the blade missed him. Jack retaliated with his fist, striking Limehouse squarely on the chin, rocking him back on his heels.

The guard staggered, attempted to catch his balance. But Jack's blow had landed unchecked. The force had driven Limehouse back so that his feet slipped in the loose rock on the brim of the ravine.

Desperately Limehouse tried to catch himself as he toppled backward through the crevice. From his lips came a scream of horror which ended with the thud of his body on the rocks below.

Limehouse had been swallowed up by the very rock which he had used to cause the doom of other men.

But Jack had no time to consider the ironic justice of his enemy's fate. The patrol plane was a growing speck in the northern sky. At its speed it soon would pass the island. There was no time to lose. Besides, other guards were steadily climbing the trail in response to the alarm given by Limehouse's pistol shots.

Negotiating the crevice with another leap, Jack ran to his home-made glider. Here was the moment on which all depended.

The sun was high enough to warm the eastern side of the mountain. The thermal updraft would do the rest.

Lifting his glider with tired muscles, Jack stood just in front of a bent piece of bamboo which was to serve as a seat. He held the glider above his head.

If the construction were scientifically correct, the make-shift flying machine would float gracefully in the air. Otherwise, Jack would end in much the same manner as Limehouse had met his fate a few minutes earlier.

Drawing a deep breath, Jack started to run.

"Here goes nothing!" he muttered.

He had a rough idea of how the Wright brothers must have felt when they made their first flight at the beginning of the century.

The wings of the glider caught the air as Jack reached the edge of the precipice overlooking the sea. A cry sounded behind. A gun cracked and a bullet whizzed past Jack's head. The guards had reached the summit and were trying to stop the fantastic escape.

Jack sprang over the edge of the precipice. The taut silken dresses strained in the air. The nose wobbled and pointed downward.

Something was wrong. The glider was in a dive. It had the gliding angle of a brick!

Jack realized what was amiss. The tail was too light.

Already he had swung his legs through the bent bamboo pole in the center of the wing, where he had intended to ride. The weight of Jack's body was sending the glider headlong toward the sea.

Hooking his knees over the pole which served as a seat, Jack leaned back, catching hold of the spars with his hands about midway between the wing and the tail. The shifting of the body weight threw the center of gravity toward the rear. The nose came up and the glider floated.

Although the glider now was soaring, Jack's troubles still were not ended. He needed all of the lessons he had learned at Elmira glider meets in order to fly this craft.

The makeshift machine actually was floating downward, but the thermal updraft from the sun-blistered rocks was strong enough to lift him faster than he fell.

There were no ailerons to steer the craft, but Jack had attached wires from his seat to the tips of the wings. He was able to make slight turns by warping the wing tips with these wires. In this manner he made the craft circle in the updraft so that gradually he rose higher and higher above the rock island.

Guards on the summit and ledges of Devil's Kitchen had spotted him and were firing madly. But their aim was bad, and Jack was slowly drifting out of range for accurate shooting.

Far away Jack saw the bomber turn in its course. It had been attracted toward the island by the sight of the weird flying machine.

Jack's one chance now was to bring the glider down

Jack Shifted His Weight to Steady the Glider

on the water so the bomber could land and pick him up before—he hoped—the sharks got him.

The glider settled downward as Jack sent it out to sea. As the craft approached the water, Jack swung forward and dived head first into the ocean. The glider splashed and floated gently on the waves.

The bomber circled the spot, and then came gently down on the water, taxiing toward the spot where Jack swam. A hatch opened and a man tossed a life preserver and rope to Jack.

A moment later, Jack was being pulled aboard the craft.

"Fellow, you sure executed an amazing feat!" exclaimed the young ensign who pulled Jack aboard the airplane.

The naval officer's eyes looked pityingly at Jack's striped prison uniform.

"—but I'm afraid it's our duty to return you to the prison from which you just escaped!"

Jack shook his head. He'd clear up everything in a few minutes.

"Listen, old man, I'm no convict!" he said. "Take me to your captain and I'll spin my yarn. This is important —as important as a big battle!"

"Bring the castaway in here!" came a voice from the cockpit.

It was a strangely familiar voice.

Jack entered the cockpit and the voice came again as a welcome roar.

"Smilin' Jack! You old son-of-a-gun!"

Seated at the controls and smiling broadly was "Downwind" Jaxon!

"Why, you old lady killer!" Jack cried, recognizing his pal.

Downwind grimaced as he saw Jack's prison uniform.

"So they finally caught up with you, eh? You old moth-eaten tail skid!"

Jack suddenly recalled that there was much important work to be done.

"Listen, Downwind," he said. "I was doing some undercover work and I've uncovered the biggest spy ring in this hemisphere. Better take off right away before the crook in charge of that prison gets on your tail!"

"Eh? So that's it, eh?" Downwind said. "What do you think we've been patrolling this island every day for? Say, Jack, this place has been under suspicion for a long time, but we haven't been able to crack the mystery—"

"I think I can explain."

An elderly, gray-haired man in civilian clothes appeared at the cockpit door.

"A man by the name of Powder Pellet, who is held in California, made a statement regarding some strange activities here. While I believe they are unfounded, I am anxious for the matter to be cleared up."

"Let me introduce you, Jack," Downwind said. "This is J. Q. Brown, owner of South American Airlines—"

"Not Betty's father!" Jack exclaimed.

"Eh? You know my daughter!"

"You bet I do and if you think there isn't anything fishy going on at this island you've got another guess coming!"

Briefly Jack explained what had happened.

"I had no idea!" Mr. Brown said. "I trusted Mr. Ghindi implicitly. I didn't suspect he was misusing my trust to carry on such nefarious schemes."

A sailor called from the forward machine-gun turret:

"Planes taking off from Death Rock!"

Downwind sprang into action. The huge bomber roared and swept across the waves, gathering speed for a take-off. As it left the water tiny pursuit planes were speeding toward it from the prison island.

Turning the controls over to the co-pilot, Downwind barked orders to the men in his command. Machine guns were manned; the radio operator was contacting head-quarters ashore to send the vital information Jack had gained to naval authorities at once, in the event that the battle should go badly.

The radio operator reported that a carrier was near-by. It was sending help, but the bomber would have to hold off the enemy until that help arrived.

Then the first wave of pursuit planes reached the bomber. The rear machine gun clattered and the leading fighter plane ducked as tracers wove a pattern across its nose.

Jack, eager to do something, found a place to watch in the gun blister just aft of the control cabin. He caught glimpses of the pursuits diving and dodging, trying to come at the huge bomber from all directions.

One enemy pursuit swept close enough for Jack to catch a glimpse of the man in the cockpit—even behind the goggles, Jack recognized the dwarfed savage little man:

The Head himself.

The pursuit ship circled and came back. Fire spat from the wings. Bullets splattered into the huge bomber. The machine gunner in the turret groaned and clapped his hand to his shoulder.

"Here, son!" Jack cried, springing to help the wounded gunner. He dragged the man away from his seat. "Patch up your wound. I'll handle this Emma Gee."

The gunner groaned his thanks as Jack took his post and trained the fifty-caliber weapon on the plane carrying The Head. The craft floated in his sights and Jack squeezed the trigger.

The gun sang a song of death as white streaks of the tracers sped true toward the mark. The little pursuit ship shuddered as bullets shredded its vitals at the rate of five slugs a second.

The enemy pursuit ship nosed downward with red tongues of flame licking upward through the fuselage. Out of control it spun downward toward the sea.

That was the end of The Head.

Another plane swam into view and Jack was busy again. The machine guns of the bomber were taking a deadly toll of its attackers. The pursuits grew wary as

two more ships crashed in flames. A third limped homeward badly damaged.

A sailor shouted joyfully from the rear turret.

"Uncle Sam's coming!"

Off to the north the sky was black with navy planes.
Nearly two score of Uncle Sam's best bombers and fight-
ers were coming to the rescue. But they were hardly
needed. Already the sea under the big bomber was litter-
ed with wreckage and the rest of the pursuits were struggling homeward.

The bomber wheeled about, making its way toward
Death Rock, leading the bombers to attack the citadel of
The Head's spy ring.

But on the turret of the prison tower a white flag was
being run up on the mast. Without The Head, the underlings of the ring were surrendering for lack of leader-
ship. They sensed that bombs from Uncle Sam's naval
planes would not strike gently.

The planes landed in the prison airfield. Pilots, battered from the recent engagement with Downwind Jaxon's patrol bomber, quickly surrendered, while Jack, Mr.
Brown and Downwind went immediately to the prison
headquarters to accept the surrender of the prison
officials.

"This is most embarrassing!" Commandant Trefwitz
exclaimed as he came face to face with Mr. Brown.

"I'll say it is!" Mr. Brown exploded. "You'd better trot
my daughter out here before I wring your dirty neck!"

"Bring Fat Stuff, too!" Jack added.

Within a few hours some drastic changes were being made on Death Rock and Devil's Kitchen. Guards now were the prisoners and several hundred convicts who had been kidnapped by hirelings of The Head were released. Only criminals actually sentenced by the government courts were held in cells, but these men were to be transferred back to the mainland to serve their time under more humane conditions. A message would be sent to apprehend the corrupt official in the governmental capital responsible for the ghastly conditions in the prison.

Within a short time an American cruiser anchored off the island. U. S. Marines landed to get the situation well in hand.

Smilin' Jack, dressed in a borrowed naval uniform, greeted Betty Brown after her father had brought her from the Kitchen.

"You look more like yourself now, Jack," Betty exclaimed joyously.

"I'm glad I don't look like 'Powder' any more!"

"I hope you never look like that man again, Jack," Betty declared, flushing. "I've got my right senses back again. I can't understand why I was so misled about the man. He had been working for my father for years, I thought—although he was actually working for The Head. He really could act like a gentleman if he wanted to. And to think, all of that time he was making his money shanghaiing unfortunate men to the living death of this island—"

"That's only a small part of it," Downwind said as he

arrived on the scene in company with Fat Stuff, who also had been released. "Did you ever see this beauty before?"

Downwind fished a gleaming object from his pocket.

"My engagement ring!" Betty exclaimed.

"I found it in The Head's safe," Downwind said. "But I recognized it from the description Powder gave to the FBI in California. That ring was stolen from a man Powder kidnaped and brought here to die—"

"That was the ring I used to cut the glass porthole and escape from the yacht," Jack said. "The Head must have found it in the clothes I left on the yacht."

"A thief, too!" Betty cried, aghast. "He didn't even mention that he had found it!"

"The stone is worth a small fortune," Downwind went on. "The American government will see that it is returned to the rightful heirs. But there's a big treasure on this island that Powder will never get to spend. It is made up of a lot of money and jewels he took from the men he kidnaped. While some of it may be returned to its owners, undoubtedly much of it will never be claimed. I think Jack ought to have some of it as a reward for bringing The Head down—"

"It's hardly fair to give me a reward. Give it to Fat Stuff," Jack said. "If it hadn't been for Fat Stuff, I might have died in the prison."

"Me buyum war bonds," Fat Stuff said simply, and grinned.

"We'll see what can be done about it," Mr. Brown said.

"But you seem to know a lot about my island that I never suspected, Downwind—"

"Powder made a pretty full confession," Downwind explained, "but the story was so wild we hesitated to act on it without corroboration—which Jack was good enough to give us."

"I understand," Mr. Brown nodded. "You hated to interfere for fear of upsetting our Good Neighbor policy by offending the country which owns this island. I think that government will be highly pleased with Uncle Sam's work in clearing up this twentieth-century slave trade on Death Rock."

"What's next, Downwind?" Jack asked.

"Well, I just got a radiogram from headquarters. I'm to bring you back to San Diego—there's another job for you to do."

"When do I leave?"

Downwind seemed to study, and then he winked at Jack.

"I wouldn't think of leaving before tomorrow," he said.

Jack grinned and took Betty by the arm.

"Did you ever see a South Sea island by moonlight?" he asked.

"Why, of course, Jack!" Betty said.

Jack looked blankly at Betty and said:

"Shucks, I thought I could show you something new—"

"Oh, but it's something I never get tired of!" Betty exclaimed. "I love to watch it from my plane when I'm flying at night!"

"If there was ever a daredevil girl pilot," Jack said enthusiastically, "you're one in a million!"

But in the back of Smilin' Jack's mind there was the pressing thought that moonlight romance was not for him—back in San Diego another assignment was waiting, and he yearned to learn what it might be.

WHITMAN
BOYS' FICTION

ADVENTURE—THRILLS—MYSTERY

Follow your **Favorite Characters** through page after page of **Thrilling Adventures.** Each book is a complete story.

Bert Wilson at Panama
Rushton Boys at Rally Hall
Joe Strong, the Boy Wizard
Bobby Blake at Rockledge School
Bobby Blake at Bass Cove
Andy Lane: Fifteen Days in the Air
Andy Lane Over the Polar Ice
Tom Slade, Boy Scout
Tom Slade at Temple Camp
Pee Wee Harris
Pee Wee Harris on the Trail
Garry Grayson's Winning Touchdown
Garry Grayson's Double Signals
Rex Cole, Jr. and the Crystal Clue
Rex Cole, Jr. and the Grinning Ghost
The Hermit of Gordon's Creek
Kidnapped in the Jungle
Rover Boys Series (4 titles)
Tom Swift Series (4 titles)
The Great Marvel Series (4 titles)

The books listed above may be purchased at the same store where you secured this book

WHITMAN
AUTHORIZED EDITIONS

NEW STORIES OF ADVENTURE AND MYSTERY

Up-to-the-minute novels for boys and girls about **Favorite Characters,** all popular and well-known, including—

Ginger Rogers and the Riddle of the Scarlet Cloak
Deanna Durbin and the Adventure of Blue Valley
Deanna Durbin and the Feather of Flame
Ann Rutherford and the Key to Nightmare Hall
Blondie and Dagwood's Secret Service
Polly the Powers Model: The Puzzle of the Haunted
    Camera
Jane Withers and the Hidden Room
Bonita Granville and the Mystery of Star Island
Joyce and the Secret Squadron: A Captain Midnight
    Adventure
Nina and Skeezix (of "Gasoline Alley") : The Prob-
    lem of the Lost Ring
Red Ryder and the Mystery of the Whispering Walls
Red Ryder and the Secret of Wolf Canyon
Smilin' Jack and the Daredevil Girl Pilot
April Kane and the Dragon Lady: A "Terry and the
    Pirates" Adventure

**The books listed above may be purchased in the same store
where you bought this book.**

WHITMAN
GIRLS' FICTION

ADVENTURE—THRILLS—MYSTERY

Follow your **Favorite Characters** through page after page of **Thrilling Adventures.** Each book is a complete story.

Joy and Gypsy Joe
Joy and Pam
Joy and Her Chum
Joy and Pam at Brookside
Judy Jordan
Judy Jordan's Discovery
Polly's Business Venture
Polly in New York
Polly at Pebbly Pit
Polly and Eleanor
Rose's Great Problem
Helen's Strange Boarder
The Outdoor Girls on a Hike
The Outdoor Girls on a Canoe Trip
The Outdoor Girls at Cedar Ridge
The Outdoor Girls in the Air